RUN OR DIE

To Savannah,

Happy Birthday!

Beth Howlett

RUN or DIE

BETH HOWLETT

TATE PUBLISHING
AND ENTERPRISES, LLC

Published by Tate Publishing & Enterprises, LLC
127 E. Trade Center Terrace | Mustang, Oklahoma 73064 USA
1.888.361.9473 | www.tatepublishing.com

Tate Publishing is committed to excellence in the publishing industry. The company reflects the philosophy established by the founders, based on Psalm 68:11,
"The Lord gave the word and great was the company of those who published it."

Book design copyright © 2014 by Tate Publishing, LLC. All rights reserved.
Cover design by Rodrigo Adolfo
Interior design by Manolito Bastasa

Published in the United States of America

ISBN: 978-1-63185-291-6
Fiction / General
14.04.25

ACKNOWLEDGMENTS

There are people without whom I would never have gotten this book off the ground. My husband, Roy, is number one in my support group. He also is my go-to person for research. I want to thank my daughter Elizabeth, my granddaughter Kaylee, and Janis Jackson for being my readers and correctors. I thank you, Tate Publishing, for giving me the opportunity to get this book on the shelves.

CHAPTER 1

"Run," he told himself, though what he was running from he couldn't remember. He just knew two things. His head hurt terribly and he needed to run. The alley was narrow and dark and dirty. How did he get here? And where was here? He felt lost and it frightened him. How could he find his way home when he couldn't remember where home was?

He caught sight of his reflection in a dirty store window. Pale blue eyes stared back at him from under a fringe of light brown hair. He didn't recognize his own face. *How could that be?* It scared him so much that he fell headlong into a pile of garbage and crates that were in a heap by the back door of the store. That was when he noticed that the door wasn't quite closed all the way. He jumped up, intending to slip inside the store, but got so dizzy all he did was land on his knees. He waited for his head to stop reeling, but the sound of running feet made him jump up and claw his way to the door. It screeched a little as he pulled at it, and the sound made him cringe. They might have heard. *They?* He had no time to think about that. He had to run.

Once inside he pulled the door all the way shut and threw the heavy bolt across to lock it. It was so dark he could almost feel the darkness envelope him. He carefully picked his way through stacked boxes and crates until he finally reached a wall. He slid his hand along the wall, looking for a way out, an opening or a door.

Air. He could feel air across his face. He traced around the wall, "Yes!" he whispered, "a door. Thank you, God." He gently tried the knob, hoping it wasn't locked. The door opened and he stepped carefully through into the back of the store. It was deserted. Late. He looked around. This had to be the kitchen of a restaurant. There were ovens and cook surfaces everywhere, and refrigerators. *Food*! He realized how hungry he was, and very thirsty. Maybe they wouldn't miss just a little. He opened the largest refrigerator but there really wasn't anything he could eat. It was all raw meat and eggs. The smaller refrigerator was filled with sandwich-type meats and vegetables. He found a loaf of bread in one of the cupboards and made himself a thick sandwich. He poured himself a large glass of milk and sat on the counter to quickly eat his bounty. When he finished, he washed the glass and put it back where he found it. No one would even know he had been here. Some day, maybe, he could come back and pay them for the food he ate.

Now, how to get out of here? He made his way to the front. Locked. *Pick it*, he told himself. *Could he do that?* He rummaged around one of the drawers in the kitchen and found a pin he could use. *Bend it like this*, he told himself. *Now, push it this way and like this*. It popped open after three tries. *How did he know to do that? Is that what he was? A criminal? Were the police after him and that's why he was running? Maybe he should give himself up. He didn't want to be a criminal.* He slipped out the front door but heard a noise at the back of the store.

Run! he told himself. *You have to run or you'll die.*

He skittered up the sidewalk as fast and as quietly as possible, ducking into another alley just a little way down. The alley led to another side street, and he kept changing streets and alleys until he was at the very edge of the town. It took a long time. He was so tired he could hardly put one foot in front of the other. And his head hurt so bad it made him feel nauseous. He had to find a safe place to rest.

What are those? He was looking toward a group of small trailers lined up a few yards apart. RVs. An RV parking area. If he could just find one unlocked where he could hide for a little while and get some rest. He was so tired.

He tried three before he found one that wasn't locked. It looked pretty large to him, and new. Maybe they didn't forget to lock it. Maybe there was someone inside. He didn't know where all the people were, but he could hear a crowd cheering loudly in the big building off in the distance. He climbed the two narrow steps into the vehicle, eased the door open as quietly as possible and made his way toward the back. The furnishings were really nice. All the cabinets were of a light colored wood and he thought the counters were real marble. Someone had decorated with frilly white curtains that had small blue flowers on them. He looked in the bathroom and at the over-the-cab compartment. No one was there. He heaved a sigh of relief. There was a small bedroom in the back. No one was there either. Poking around, he finally found a small closet that wasn't quite stuffed full. He slipped in to see if he had enough room.

Not great, but I can manage, he thought. He was almost asleep when it hit him. He needed to use the bathroom. He opened the door a crack and looked out. No one was there, so he slipped out and used the bathroom. Before he got back in the closet, he grabbed a couple of bottles of water from the refrigerator. He also took two slices of bread from the loaf on the counter. Maybe they wouldn't miss what little he took. He took a couple of sips of water and put the rest in the corner next to him. Within seconds he was sound asleep, not even waking up when the owners returned and started up the big engine.

CHAPTER 2

A couple of times when the RV stopped the boy would quickly slip to the bathroom, grab a bottle of water and a banana from the kitchen, and be back in his hiding place. He didn't even take time to look out the little window. Mostly he just slept. He felt so tired. Each time the couple returned the lingering aroma of food would tease his nose. Instead of making him hungry it made him feel sick. His head still hurt and felt strange. Like it didn't belong to him. A long while later he woke up again. He had no idea how long he had been asleep and no clue where he was. He gently opened the door, sure that any second it was going to squeak and give him away. The RV was stopped at a small gas station. How far had they gone? Nothing looked like it did before he went to sleep. There were very few trees and not very many buildings. It was so hot, stifling hot. *Where was this?* He tried to peek out a window to see if he could see the people who owned the RV, but all he saw was sand and some kind of plant with arms.

The heat was making him so thirsty. He had just reached into the refrigerator when a loud voice said, "What are you doing there, young man?"

"I...I...just..." he stammered, unable to come up with an explanation.

"Marian, call the police. We have a thief."

"Please, please don't. I'll leave."

"Yeah, you'll leave and go down to the next RV or house to do your stealing. Well, we're going to put an end to your criminal career right now."

"I...I don't think I'm a criminal. I don't want to be. I only took a couple of pieces of bread and some water. Please, I'll pay you back." Then he realized he didn't have any money. All he had was a small camera in his pocket.

"I don't have any money," he said so softly the man barely heard him. The man took a closer look and what he saw almost broke his heart. This was just a very young boy. Not near as old as his size indicated. He motioned Marian closer to him. "Get the boy something to eat." He lifted the boy's head with his hand so he could look him in the eye. Nice looking young man. Clear eyes...good skin.

"Tell me the truth now, boy. How long have you been in our RV?"

"I can't remember and I think I fell asleep, so I don't know how long ago it was. But it looks different here. When I got in there were trees all around and no sand."

"What's your name?"

"I...I...I'm not sure. I can't think of it right now."

"Okay…where do you live?" He hoped it wasn't too far. He wanted to get to the next RV park before it was filled up for the night. Taking turns driving, they had driven straight through to Phoenix, but he just had to get some rest.

By the blank look on his face, he knew the boy had no clue where he lived.

"Well, we've got to find the police station so they can get you home."

"No! Please. I…please don't. I'll leave. Just don't take me to the police."

"Micah, let the boy clean up while I fix him some food. He looks starved," Marian said as she handed the boy a towel and pointed toward the bathroom. She couldn't stand the thought of a child being hungry.

He felt a little better after showering in the tiny RV shower. His head was a little better, but it still hurt. He thought of the man and woman. At first the man seemed terrifying. His voice was so loud it made his head start hurting again. His size matched his voice. Big. Muscular and kind of hairy, but no longer a young man. Not old, really, just not young. The woman, probably his wife, had such a kind face. She must smile a lot, because there were a few lines around her mouth. *Laugh lines* he thought they were called. She was short, a little chubby, kind of like Mrs. Santa Claus. She even had the rosy cheeks.

While he was in the shower and couldn't overhear them, the couple talked it over and decided not to turn the boy over to the police. "If he's a runaway, something must be very wrong with his home life. He sounded so frightened."

"He belongs somewhere, Marian. He probably got in trouble and ran away from home." He looked toward the back of the RV and saw the open closet door. He looked inside at the two empty plastic water bottles. The boy had been in the closet, probably for quite a while. No telling where he was from. He pointed it out to his wife. "He's been in that closet for some time, I bet."

"Why can't he remember his name, or where he lives?" Micah had no answer for that. "Please let's just let him stay awhile. Til he calms down."

The man hugged his wife. Her expression softened as the boy came back into the room. "We'll give it a couple of days. See how he reacts. Maybe he'll be ready to go home by then." It was probably a mistake, but the beaming smile on his wife's face was worth it.

CHAPTER 3

The boy had been with them for almost two weeks. They had stayed a couple of days in Arizona then moved on to take in the sights in Colorado and Wyoming. Whenever they stopped at a campsite, he would help them set up the RV. He had proven himself to them. He was a fast learner and a hard worker. He never complained when things went wrong, just worked harder to get them right. His quick wit and sense of humor kept the couple entertained for hours at a time. Micah could tell that his wife was beginning to form an attachment to the boy. Her mothering instincts were in full force. He knew that he, too, was seeing the boy more as their son. The son they had lost contact with.

No one knew about their son. They had been too ashamed to say anything about the reasons he had left home. All the drugs and things. So they said nothing to their friends. Just pretended he was away at school. With all their traveling around the country it was easy to cover the fact that they hadn't seen their son in over a year.

Micah had thought about it a lot. Maybe the boy could stay with them. They had brought up the subject of going to the police several times, but the boy would get so agitated, they finally gave up. If he stayed with them, they could protect him from an abusive home life…and they could have a son again.

"Marian." She looked over at the man who had been her husband, her lover, and her friend for so many years. She nodded. He didn't have to say anything. They had each come to the same place.

"A son, Micah. Can we do this? Would God forgive us?"

"How do we know that God didn't put us in this boy's life to help him?" was her husband's answer.

"We can give him so much. Love and a good home. Knowledge. We can teach him so many things." Micah knew his wife had missed their son so much. Not just because he had left them a year ago. He began to pull away from them a couple of years before that. They knew it was because of the crowd he ran around with. That gang. Didn't make them love him any less. They just couldn't hold onto him.

It was true that they could provide a good life for this boy. They had been professors at MIT for several years. She taught chemistry and physics and her husband taught several technical courses. They had used their combined knowledge to invent. One invention was a nanobot that could infiltrate enemy territory and sniff out certain chemical weapons and bomb materials without their presence being detected. They also invented an important improvement on the night vision and infrared goggles that were worn by military as well as SWAT teams. A small item they sold to the government was another nanobot. This one could carry a small detector into a wounded soldier's body and quickly pinpoint shrapnel for the doctors to take out without the need for ex-rays. They sold schematics for a revolutionary type of chip to a computer company for a *lot* of money. It was enough that they could retire from teaching and travel around the country.

"Son, we don't know what all you've been through but it looks like you may have been abused. We would like to help you but we can't find any reports in the papers about you being missing. Do you want us to take you to the police so they can help you?"

"No. No, please don't. Can I just stay here? I promise I won't eat much, and I'll stay out of your way. Please?" He was almost hysterical by this time.

"Son…it's okay. Take it easy. We're on your side. Okay?" Micah could see the boy visibly relax. A smile lit up the boy's face. *Probably would be a heartbreaker as he got older*. Micah had never heard the boy use any foul language the way so many young people do today.

"Now, there are some things we'll have to do to make this work. Are you willing to do what we say?" At the boy's quick nod, Micah went on. "Alright. We'll be straight up with you if you'll do the same with us." Another nod from the boy. "We have, or had, a son. He left home a year ago and we've not heard from him since. We think he may be dead. We just don't know. We have missed him so much. If we treat you as our son, would you think of us as your parents? It wouldn't have to be forever, just until your memory comes back. We want you to be honest with us. If you remember anything, anything at all, you'll tell us. Okay?"

"We're only guessing about your loss of memory but that's what it looks like."

"How would I have lost it?" Then he shook his head. "Of course. There's no way you could know."

Micah realized that this young boy was pretty levelheaded for his apparent age. He had accepted what Micah asked and was now analyzing it. After several minutes went by, the boy looked up at Micah and Marian and asked, "What's your son's name?"

"Camden, but we always called him Cam."

"What will you call me?"

"What would you like to be called?"

"Would 'Mike' be okay?"

Micah Calloway could only nod. The lump in his throat wouldn't allow him to speak.

CHAPTER 4

Finally, after site seeing in several states, they headed to California, to their home in San Diego. They had a small but beautifully decorated two-bedroom cottage on Coronado Island. The beach off the island was one of the best in the state. Mike loved the beach and would stay out there for hours on end just surfing and swimming. His hair was so bleached from the sun it was almost silver and his skin had a dark tan even after using the sunscreen his mom insisted on. Sometimes his parents would come to the beach with him and they would have a cookout. They always took the opportunity to teach him about things, and they made it fun at the same time. They taught him what the different shells were called and where they came from originally. Micah showed him how to snorkel. They took classes on deep sea diving until Mike was proficient and knew all the safety precautions by heart.

Mike loved his "parents." They were a bit older than you would expect them to be if they really were his parents but they were loving and kind. They were patient with him, showing him how to do things again if he didn't quite understand at first. His "dad" taught him how to take care of all their vehicles. Taught him how to change the oil, fix a flat, clean and weatherize the RV. They taught him how to manage their finances. Secretly, his favorite thing he learned was how to cook. Really cook. His mom could have been a master chef in any big time restaurant. She would tell him, "You never know when you may need to take care of yourself. You can't eat out all the time. It's not healthy."

Life was good.

But something always seemed…missing. He knew he must have another family somewhere. Were they missing him or were they just glad he was gone? Were they heartbroken at the loss of their son or had they been abusive, causing him to seek shelter with the Calloways? Perhaps he would never know unless his memory returned.

CHAPTER 5

They spent some time at their home in California, but they still took the RV on trips around the country. They also spent several vacations in other countries. Micah and Marian explained the history of each country and taught Mike about the different cultural values of each place they visited. They were amazed how quickly Mike picked up the languages. He had proved to be an amazing boy. He was highly intelligent, had a fun sense of humor, was well mannered, and very protective of his "parents." He had learned at least two different martial arts styles just so he would be able to take care of any situation that might come up. So that he could protect them. They loved him so much. He was so different from Cam. Cam had been the typical child growing up, but he had never wanted to accept the things his parents wanted to teach him. To him they were just "old" people. He sought out his friends for advice instead of his parents. Maybe they had been too lenient with him, allowed him too much freedom trying to make up for having him so late in their lives. They didn't realize until it was too late that Cam had drifted so far from them.

His values had been corrupted by his friends' bad influences. He became increasingly upset with them for asking about where he was going and what he was doing out so late. They knew he was headed for trouble, but by then they were powerless to control his movements.

One morning they woke up early and found his bedroom door open, his bed never slept in, dresser drawers pulled out with some clothing missing. It broke their hearts to lose their only child. Marian went in and straightened the drawers, made the bed, and sat down on it. She cried and prayed for hours that God would keep him safe and bring him back to them.

CHAPTER 6

After two years of home schooling by both of the Calloways, Mike was ready to go on to college. He had absorbed everything they could teach him, which was considerable, as well as things he picked up on his own. He had the credits he needed from all the online courses and had taken all the tests required. His scores were off the charts. Since he didn't need scholarship money, he could essentially choose any college or university he wanted to attend.

During the two years with Micah and Marian, he had remembered only one thing. Soon after he agreed to be their son, they wanted him to get a driver's license in order to help Micah with driving the RV. It was after they had gone with him to take his driving test to get his license. (Mike didn't know how his parents had come up with a birth certificate for him, but they had.) He had passed his test and could expect his license in the mail in a few weeks.

Why this made him remember was anyone's guess, but he remembered how old he was. He was twelve at that time. They had known he was younger than their son, but they didn't think it was that much. Their son was sixteen.

What about the college? Will they be able to tell that I'm not old enough? Will they be able to tell I'm only fourteen? He really wanted to go to college. He liked learning and wanted to make his parents proud of him.

"You'll have a birth certificate and a driver's license to prove that you're almost eighteen. Who could argue?" Micah hoped his words were enough to comfort his son. His son. This boy was not his biological son, but he couldn't love him more if he was his own real flesh and blood. He knew that Marian felt the same, maybe even more so. He was such a good kid. The thought of him being away at college was hard. But they had prepared him very well. Not just his mind, but his heart. Wherever they were on their travels, they went to the nearest church that shared their faith. When they were home they went to their church. Mike would always be up and dressed early on Sunday morning. He loved hearing the messages about the Savior, and he loved singing the hymns. He brought up the subject of going into the ministry to his parents, but they explained that going into the ministry was not a choice you made, but one God made. You had to be called into the ministry, otherwise you would not be able to stand the pressures and temptations that came from all different directions. They told him to pray about it and God would provide an answer.

CHAPTER 7

Two years later Mike graduated with honors from Cal Tech in California. His parents had wanted him to go to MIT, but he didn't want to be that far away from them. During those two years he remembered only a couple of things about his past life. He remembered his sisters – not their names – just the fact that he had two older sisters, but he couldn't remember if he had any younger sisters. The other thing he remembered was his camera, the one he had with him when the Calloways found him, or rather when he found them.

He picked it up during one of his visits home and took it to a print shop to get the film developed. The technician, a young man with blue hair and many tattoos, said he thought the film might be okay. Maybe a little yellowed but clear enough.

The photography tech, Drew, gave him a weird look when he came to pick up the pictures the next day. Apparently he had given them the once over while he was processing them.

"Dude, there's no charge. I could only get three or four pictures to come out. I can try some enhancement of the others and…maybe…get a couple more, if ya want."

Mike couldn't figure out at first what the pictures were about. They just showed some men in an alley. It was dark and you couldn't see very much about them except for one that was facing the camera and a light from somewhere streaked across his face. The man looked familiar to Mike but he just couldn't remember from where. What he could also see was the man had on a policeman's uniform and was pointing a gun at one of the other men. That man was down on his knees with his hands out like he was begging with the other man not to shoot him. Another picture showed the kneeling man crumpled on the ground. Mike felt a chill run down his back.

"That's okay. This will be fine. Thanks for your help."

"Anytime, man." As Mike left the little photo shop, 'Drew Something' gave him another funny look then went back to his processing.

Mike felt the pictures needed to be kept somewhere safe. Maybe it was because they were all he had from his previous life. He rented a safety deposit box at a bank in Pasadena. He put the photos inside with a brief note and his name and address on it. He never thought to show them to his parents or ask their advice. As he was driving away from the bank, he thought he would bring his parents to Pasadena and show them the pictures. Maybe they could advise him on what to do. He called them on his way home but they were busy taking care of some business. They said they would call him back in a little while. He stopped to eat at a quaint little diner set just off the interstate. He expected they would call about the time he got his mouth full of food. It surprised him that he was finished eating and back on the road and there was still no call.

Micah and Marian had been to the their bank and now they were leaving their lawyer's office. Marian had insisted that she and Micah needed to make sure their financial papers were in order. Micah had tried to put her off. He didn't like to think about those things.

"You're right, Marian. They needed done and this way you will be able to relax and enjoy the rest of the day with me." His wife smiled and reached for his hand as they passed in front of a building that was under construction. A terrible screeching from above caused them to stop and look up.

Several bystanders were hurt from flying debris when the huge crane fell from the top of the building.

Mike heard the sirens as he passed near the street where it looked like the emergency vehicles were headed. He couldn't see what was going on but he felt a strange sensation in the pit of his stomach. He tried to call his parents again. When there was still no answer, he knew. *Something's happened to them.*

One other person had been seriously injured in the incident, but they survived. His parents didn't. The worst day of Mike's life, that he could remember, was going to the morgue to make a positive identification of his parents' bodies. He knew where they were now, and that they were happy to be with their Savior, but he was going to miss them so much. Every memory of them came crashing down on him. How they took him in, taught him things, *loved* him. He felt weighted down with sorrow. He knew life had to go on, another thing they had taught him. They also taught him how to deal with every burden, every sorrow. "Take it to Jesus," they would say. "Lay it at His feet." And that's what he did.

CHAPTER 8

The company the crane belonged to had already been warned about their shoddy handling of equipment. Other accidents had happened the last year, but the company refused to spend the money to put in the necessary safeguards.

The company balked at paying the money. They said it wasn't their fault. Their lawyers were well paid to keep their clients out of hot water, but this time they had met their match with Mike's lawyer.

Mike didn't really want the money that the company settled for. He was talked into it by his parents' lawyer. Of course the lawyer wanted to sue for several million dollars, but Mike insisted on settling for a reasonable amount. Even that amount, two million dollars, was way more than Mike wanted it to be, but the lawyer had insisted that the amount was reasonable. The company could afford it and someone needed to impress on them the need to change their ways. If they kept getting off lightly, they would never change and someone else could get hurt in the future. That argument helped Mike to accept the lawyer's pleas. To Mike, no amount of money could take away the hurt of losing his beloved Micah and Marian.

Going home after their funeral, he felt so lost and alone. The place was so quiet, so empty – he couldn't stand it. He took a blanket and walked down to the beach and spent the night. For a while he just felt numb, but the waves crashing and the smell of the ocean on the night air finally reached him. He let the tears flow unchecked down his face. He prayed until, finally, a peace came over him and he slept under the silver moon and caressing night breeze.

CHAPTER 9

In his parents' private papers, Mike found a document. It outlined everything that had happened with the boy they took into their home and their hearts. They left everything to him, all their property and personal items. It stated that their lawyer also had a sealed copy of the letter. He looked at the date on the paperwork. It was dated less than three months after he started living with them. They had provided for him in case something happened to them. When he talked with the lawyer a few days later, the lawyer explained the will that the Calloways had updated just in the last year. He explained the additions they had made on the day of their deaths. Everything they had was left to Mike, whoever Mike turned out to be if or when his memory came back.

There was one provision. If their son Camden was still alive and ever came back, the will had set aside one million dollars in a trust fund. If he didn't come back within ten years after their deaths, the money would transfer to Mike or Mike's heirs at the time. The lawyer gave Mike his condolences and said if he needed anything, just call. The Calloways were not just clients. They had been personal friends of his and he would miss them as well.

CHAPTER 10

Mike was devastated by his parents' death. Now he was once again, all alone with nowhere to turn. True, he was older. He had been to college, but he was still only sixteen years old. He had concentrated so hard on his studies that he had made few friends and none that he considered close. He had no family, at least that he could recall, and no one to confide in or ask advice. In some ways he felt older than his years, and in other ways he felt like a young frightened boy with no one to share his fears until a still, small voice reminded him that he could always take his fears to God. He listened to that voice and the burden of fear was lifted like a curtain. He would forever miss his parents, but they had prepared him for life and he wanted to live his life in a manner that would have made them proud. His father had told him stories of his experiences in the army. He had been proud to serve his country, proud of the Purple Heart he had earned. He even hinted at the unofficial service to his country after his official tour had ended. He had instilled a sense of honor and love of country into his son. Mike had some decisions to make. He had enjoyed college, but right now he need more purpose in his life. He had watched as many of his classmates left wives and sometimes children to go and fight for their country. He had talked about going into the military straight out of high school, but his parents begged him to go to college first.

He decided he didn't want to go to college anymore right then, so he thought he might try the military. There was a recruitment office close to the college. He had passed it every day going to and from school. He had checked out the placards about serving your country and he liked the idea. But he had been concentrating on his studies at the time and was not ready for military service. For one thing, he didn't want to be that far from his parents. But now seemed like the perfect time. He prayed about it and felt God was guiding him in that direction. He was just a little afraid that something would come up about his identification, especially his birth certificate, since it wasn't really his at all. But if God was guiding him, he didn't need to worry about that or anything else.

Mike went to the Marine recruiting office near the Cal-Tech campus and waited his turn to talk to the beefy Marine recruiter. The recruiter in his perfectly starched uniform and highly shined shoes was a good advertisement for joining the military. He signed all the papers that were shoved in front of him. He listened as they explained what military life would be like, how he might be far from home but that his fellow soldiers would become his family. He hoped that was true because right then he felt like he had no one.

CHAPTER 11

Because of his college background and language skills he was accepted into the OCS (Officer Candidate School). He completed all the steps required by the OSO (Officer Selection Officer), the interview, the essay about why he wanted to be a Marine officer, the five letters of recommendation and, the one that had him worried- the background check. He easily passed the required physical. All his information was sent to the review board and they voted to accept him into the Officer Candidate Program.

His classes consisted of academic instruction as well as field skills. He excelled at both. After the ten-week course, he was commissioned as a Second Lieutenant and went to The Basic School at Quantico for the six months of further training.

At his graduation, he felt the absence of his parents like a balloon in his chest. He fought hard not to let his eyes mist over as he watched friends and families hug and congratulate his fellow classmates. Several came over to hug him as well, making him feel not quite as alone. He had met many of the parents at different functions over the months and they knew of his parents' deaths. He had accepted several invitations to dinner at different cadets' homes. His popularity with the cadets could stem from the fact that he had invited several of them to his house and had cooked some of his famous meals for them. He had a reputation with the cadets as being something of a mystery. He could cook like a gourmet chef, but his martial arts training was impressive. Also, Mike had helped several of them in their studies. There were only a couple of the cadets that held themselves aloof from the others. They were the General's son and the son of a long-running Congressman who had made a name for himself in military service. These two boys held themselves as superior to the other cadets. They were always trying to pick on Mike, but for some reason they seemed a little leery of him. Lonnie, the General's son, hated every time Mike made a better grade on a paper or in their training exercises. He would glare at Mike and occasionally shove him when passing. It went un-noticed by the training officers and, eventually, since he couldn't get Mike to respond, he gave it up.

After his training was complete, he spent most of his four-year term in the hot spots of the Middle East. Because of his courage and leadership under fire, he caught the attention of the brass and they put him on the fast track for promotion. He was well liked by the men in his unit and tried to be the best leader possible for their sakes. His team took on some of the more clandestine operations and quickly made a name for themselves as one of the elite outfits in the military.

His last two-year tour abroad was a rough one. He had made a lot of friends over his years in the military, some of them officers and some just infantry recruits. A couple of those friends were killed in a raid on what intelligence said was the hiding place of one of the most sought after terrorist leaders of the Al Qaeda. The mission had been well planned but something had gone wrong. The terrorist leader had left just a few seconds before the raid happened, almost as if he had been warned. Mike had not been told of the leader's escape until it was too late to call off the raid. It was a justified raid and accomplished much. They had rounded up an impressive bunch of minor terrorist leaders, just not the main one they had wanted. He knew it was viewed as a good mission even with the loss of two of their men. Mike could not see it that way. None of their men should have been killed or even injured. It was typical of Mike not to even include his own injury. One of the terrorists had gotten off a lucky shot. It seemed as if he had been waiting just for Mike to come through.

It was just an in and out through the left side, not hitting any organs, just tearing up some muscle, but he had lost a fair amount of blood. He wanted to go straight back to his unit from the hospital, but the military doctors said different. They put him on R&R for six weeks.

He was back in the states on light duty for a month, so he decided to do some sightseeing around D.C. He had never been to the White House before, at least not that he knew of.

He decided to get a ticket for one of the White House tours so he could ask questions. One of the men in his company was the son of a Congressman and he was able to pull a few strings to get the ticket for him quickly.

CHAPTER 12

At the entrance to the White House, Mike followed the line of people handing in their tickets to a young man who was standing just inside the entrance. He handed his ticket over when it was his turn and the young man told him to enjoy the tour and pointed him toward the waiting tour guide.

Mike scanned the small crowd around him as they listened to the pretty young girl who was their guide. Most of the people in the group were couples with young children, a few older couples, and one or two alone like him, but older women.

He listened as the tour guide (*Randi?*) went through the history of the White House and why it was located in Washington D.C. Mike was filled with a feeling of pride and ownership. As she moved on to the next room, she gave some background on the men who had served as president of the United States, from George Washington, John Adams, and Abraham Lincoln to Ronald Regan.

When she got to the current president, Cole Harris, Randi pointed to a picture at the end of the gallery.

Mike really couldn't see it that well, but the man looked vaguely familiar. Not just familiar because he had seen the man on television, but he could almost hear the man's voice in his head. Before he could really pin anything down, Randi was having them move on to the next area. Something about that picture continued to bother him the rest of the tour.

It didn't bother him so much that it kept him from noticing how beautiful Randi was. How her hair seemed to shimmer and her smile lit up the whole room. He couldn't take his eyes off her. He asked a couple of questions, partly to get her attention and partly because he wanted to know the answers. He wanted to ask her about her name, but not in front of everyone. He couldn't get over how tongue-tied he felt. He had never been so attracted to a girl. Oh, he had dated a little. Some of the cadets would fix him up with a sister or cousin of theirs, but he had never even had a crush on one of them. He was a healthy male and had felt the usual hormones take over a time or two, but he had never let them get out of control. He knew God had someone special just for him. He didn't want to do anything to hinder God's plan for his life.

Mike was staying at a hotel on D.C.'s outer rim. He really needed to find an apartment he could settle down in and make his home base. Maybe he could ask Randi to help him find a place. *Yeah, right.* He knew it was just an excuse to talk to her, but he didn't care.

With the tour over, people started leaving out the front exit. Several stopped and complimented Randi on the tour. One little boy, with carrot red hair and a lot of freckles, said something about her name being a boys' name. She just smiled that winning smile and explained that her name was spelled Randi with an *i*.

An older woman said, "Your parents must have wanted a boy."

"Actually, I have three older brothers. I think they ended up naming me."

Mike held back as the last of the group moved on. Finally he was near Randi, and up close she looked even more fantastic. All of a sudden he was extremely nervous. He wasn't sure his voice wouldn't squeak when he tried to talk.

"Hi." That was all that would come out because at that moment Randi looked up into his eyes and whatever else he was going to say disappeared from his mind.

"Hi," was all that Randi said. She went to move away, but he finally found his voice.

"Randi, could I ask you something?" he began, but she cut him off.

"If you are going to ask me out, please, save your breath. I don't date people I meet during tours."

"No... well yes, I was going to ask you out, but since that's not an option, let me ask you this instead. Do you know of any apartments for rent around the D.C. area? Reasonably priced apartments."

Randi looked at the young man in front of her. He was very nice looking, tall, broad shoulders, narrow waist. His tan chinos and a dark blue button-up shirt showed off his muscular body. Military for sure. She was tempted, very tempted, to flirt with him, but she knew that was not a good idea. Her brothers were constantly warning her about guys around Washington.

"Sorry, I don't know of any offhand." At least she softened the letdown with a smile. He watched her walk away and had to fight off the inclination to follow her.

As Randi walked away, she thought about her parents. Her Mother, Carmen Rae, was an interpreter, mostly for the White House, but she would do other interpreting jobs where she was needed. Tully Rae, her father, was Ambassador to Israel for many years. They had lived in and around Washington D.C. for a long time and knew many of the Senators and Congressmen that frequented the White House.

Randi's parents had been at a conference in Switzerland when she was born. There was a dinner the night before the start of the conference and the Raes went but declined the after dinner drinks and dancing. Of course everyone understood considering her advanced condition. They wouldn't have gone anyway, since they didn't drink and cared little for dancing. They had an early night together instead and that suited Carmen just fine since she was a little more tired than normal. Her husband figured it was jet lag.

CHAPTER 13

The Raes' little girl let it be known she was on her way right in the midst of the conference. The pains started gradually early that morning and by the noon lunch break it was evident Carmen wasn't going to be able to finish the conference. The pains were already down to about seven minutes apart. She, and her husband Tully, barely made it to the hospital in time for their beautiful little girl to make her appearance. All the nurses *ooh'd* and *ah'd* over the precious little baby girl with the angelic face and huge blue eyes.

They stayed a couple of days in the hospital and were pronounced perfectly healthy by the doctor who signed the release papers. The nurses lined the hallway to wish them well and see the sweet little baby one more time. The Raes thanked them for all their wonderful care.

The Raes flew back home to the States a few days later and picked up the boys from Tully's parents in Boston. The boys stared at the tiny bundle with the pale blonde hair and promptly named her Randy. They thought they were going to have a little brother.

Carmen and Tully agreed it was a perfect name…if the *y* was changed to an *i*.

The boys adored their little sister and took turns holding her. Even as she got older, they didn't mind her tagging along with them, and each one watched out for her, waiting for her to catch up if she lagged behind.

They still watched out for her, even though she was almost twenty. That was okay with Randi, except sometimes they seemed to forget she wasn't a little girl anymore.

CHAPTER 14

Mike finally resorted to answering ads for apartments. Some of the apartments were outrageously priced for one room. Of course, he could afford any of them, but he wanted to live according to what he made from his military pay. He didn't want to touch the other money right now, if ever.

There were a few ads for one-bedroom apartments. On one, the girl just wanted someone to share her bedroom. No way. That wasn't for him. A couple of rooms were in the middle of the downtown district and, a couple were in slum areas. There was one ad that sounded very promising.

Two young men were sharing a three-bedroom apartment and needed a man to take up payment on the third room. The apartment was in a really nice area...close to a park. It sounded perfect. He loved to run to keep in shape and he liked to look at something other than asphalt.

Mike wasn't sure he wanted to be in such close quarters with anyone else, but something just seemed right about this. He made note of the address because he didn't want to call. He wanted to see the apartment and actually meet the other two men before he made up his mind.

Just as Mike reached out to knock on the apartment door, the door flew open and two young men almost barreled him over.

"Whoa…hey there. Sorry. We're late."

"That's okay. I was just going to ask about the room. I can come back some other time."

"Hey! Fantastic. We will be back around noon. Feel free to go in and check it out, just lock the door on your way out. It's the last room on the left."

The two young men looked to be about mid-twenties, tall, well built. Definitely related. Both had brown hair and brown eyes. Not twins but close in age.

Very trusting of a stranger, Mike thought as he looked through the apartment.

Nice kitchen. Clean with no dirty dishes around. The bedroom for rent was nice. Not too small. It had a soft dark blue carpet with curtains that had a matching stripe running through them. The window had a really nice view of the park that was close by. He peeked into the other two bedrooms, trying to size up the young men he would be living with. The beds were made and the rooms were tidy.

He checked the refrigerator. It was a nice size side-by-side and very clean. *No beer? Wow. Maybe they were just out.* He hoped that was not the case, but he knew most young men drank to some degree.

God, is this the place? I want to be where you want me.

He poked around the common living area for a minute, noticing the basket of books and magazines by the sofa. One book caught his eye. A large Bible commentary. *Thank you God. I get the message.*

He locked the door and headed down the street to find someplace to while away the three hours until noon. Maybe he could find an Internet café.

CHAPTER 15

Dan and Randi were waiting for Jeff and Will at the church to set everything up for the youth rally on Saturday. Jeff was trying not to drive too fast, but he knew Randi would chew off his ear about being late. *Well not literally,* he hoped.

"Hey, bro. Should we have just let that guy roam through our apartment?" Will was holding on to his seat as if he could make the car go faster if he picked it up and ran with it.

"Why not, Jeff? What's he gonna take?"

"Right. You have a point."

"Yay! You finally decided to show up to work." Randi gave her brothers her most stern look, which had little impact on them, since they knew she was just as happy to see them as they were to see her. They each put an arm around her and gave her a hug. Dan looked at his siblings indulgently. He loved his brothers, but he doted on his little sister. The Rae family was very close. Even though they picked at each other constantly, it was always done with love. Anybody else picking on them would bring the full ire of the whole family down on them.

"At least we're here, and ready to work. Let's get after it. We need to be back by noon. We might have someone to rent the extra room." Will fluffed the top of her hair.

Slapping at his hand, Randi gave him a questioning look.

"What happened to what's-his-name-Tony?"

"Oh. Didn't we tell you? He got married. His wife would like for him to live with her."

"Who's the guy moving in?"

"Possibly moving in. We don't know. He came by just as we were leaving to come here. Told him to go in and check it out and we would be back at noon."

Randi looked so horrified both brothers burst out laughing.

"I can't believe you left a perfect stranger alone in your apartment!"

"Hmm. I'm not sure I would call him perfect. Will, would you call him perfect?"

"Nah. Though Randi might think so. You know how she likes men in uniform. Not that he was in uniform at the time. But he looked military. Good posture close haircut...waving a bayonet." He laughed at Randi's expression. "Okay, maybe he wasn't waving a bayonet."

"Okay, guys. Very funny. *You* are the ones warning me away from dating anyone in the military."

"True. We just don't want you to get hurt, Randi. We're protective because we care about you. You're our baby sister."

"Okay! Okay. I get the idea." She gave them a glare, but it was spoiled by the smile she couldn't keep off her face.

"Go, you guys. We have a lot to get done," she said as she pushed both of her brothers toward the utility room to get supplies.

Jeff and Will left to get the tools to hang a banner for the rally and Randi gazed after them with laughter dancing in her eyes. They were a hoot.

CHAPTER 16

Mike got back to the apartment just before noon, but nobody was home yet. He leaned against the outer wall to wait and thought about the girl at the White House. Randi. How was he going to get her attention? He really liked what he saw. *Was she not interested at all, or, was she already involved with someone?*

He was so deep in thought that he didn't realize the two guys were standing right in front of him.

"Oh. Hi."

"Hey. Did you check it out?"

"Yes, I'll take it... if that's okay."

"Don't you want to know how much?" Will looked at him with suspicion in his eyes.

"Yeah, sure. I'm sure it will be reasonable though."

"Four hundred a month. But there are some guidelines, too. You may change your mind." Jeff was more the businessman than Will so he had come up with the rules that would keep the atmosphere of the apartment good for the youth that gathered there on a regular basis. They had made mistakes already and they didn't

want to make any more. The young people they men-
tored were too easily led astray as it was.

"If you smoke, you have to do it outside. Absolutely
no drugs or liquor in this apartment, and no being under
the influence while in the apartment. No female…
ahem…or male companions in the apartment." Jeff
tried to judge how his words were being received, but
his gaze was met with a blank face.

Oh well, he thought, *guess we lost this one.*

"When can I move in?"

Will and Jeff looked at each other and grinned.

"How about now?"

Mike put his things away in his bedroom and bathroom. He had some other clothing and personal
items he would bring as soon as he could get away to
California to pick them up. He didn't know whether to
keep the house or not. He hated the thought of giving
it up, but he couldn't keep a very close eye on it from
across the country.

He brought a few things for the kitchen and found
plenty of room for them in the cabinets. He didn't want
to crowd the other two guys, but he wanted to contribute his share. And he could tell from his quick perusal
earlier in the day that their kitchen lacked a few basic
tools that he could easily provide. He planned on doing
a lot of cooking at home.

He knew God was looking out for him. The rules
showed the kind of men Jeff and Will were. Mature

minded, moral men. He had missed that close associa-
tion with other godly men while in the military. Not
that there weren't some very good men, even godly men.
Just, in his unit there were none that focused on a relationship with Jesus. He had talked with many of them,
sharing his faith. A few had come to know Christ as a
result, but they had a long way to go in their personal
relationship with Jesus. That took time and studying
God's Word.

CHAPTER 17

Jeff and Will met Randi just as she got out of her car to go into Dan's house. Dan's house was a nice two story brick in an upscale neighborhood just outside the city. He invited his siblings to his house about once a week. He enjoyed their company and they all got together and fixed a meal to share. Tonight they were having steaks grilled out on the patio.

Dan opened the door before they could knock and welcomed them inside.

"Did you rent the extra room?" Randi addressed the question to Jeff, but Will answered.

"Sure did. Jeff gave him the price, then laid down all the rules. Guy didn't even bat an eye. Just asked when he could move in."

Dan looked over at his brothers, "Did he tell you much about himself?"

Jeff and Will looked at each other sheepishly.

"Great. You didn't even ask."

"He seemed like a clean cut guy. Didn't quibble about the price or the rules at all."

"That was the main interest? Renting the room for the price you wanted?" Dan just shook his head. What was he going to do with these two? The last one to rent the room had been okay. A little sloppy. Sometimes not contributing as much as he took from the apartment. But generally acceptable. Before that there had been a couple of really bad choices and one total jerk.

"I think he's military."

Randi couldn't believe her ears. "The last military man that rented the room was an insufferable creep. Or have you forgotten all he did to you? To me? To that young boy, who is now in rehab after a year on drugs. Drugs he got from that army private."

"I'm sorry Ran, we didn't think about that. Wow, what do we do now? He's already moving in."

They looked so contrite Randi couldn't help it. She reached over and grabbed each one by the hand. "Pray about it, right now, that this one will be different."

Jeff led out in a prayer about the situation and a prayer for guidance in the future. He felt a lot better just giving everything over to God. He realized that he had jumped into a situation without even consulting God. Jeff made a vow to remind himself to call on God first, not in hindsight.

CHAPTER 18

Mike heard Jeff and Will come in sometime after he had gone to bed. He didn't usually go to bed before ten or eleven, but he had early plans for the next morning. He had an appointment at the White House. Since he was still considered in recovery from his injuries, he was being assigned to a new post. One that he wasn't sure he was going to like at all. Bodyguard? It was supposed to be a light duty assignment, but he wondered if there was something else behind the job that he didn't know about.

He had answered all the questions, and they were extensive, had the personality profile, tests, everything. A full background check would be done before they assigned him the job. It would probably be a couple of weeks. There was only one thing left, and for some reason he dreaded it the most. He had to be vetted by the family, including the president himself. Tomorrow evening he was supposed to go to the White House to meet with President Harris. If the president liked him, then he would meet with the rest of the First

Family. That must mean he would be bodyguard to one of them. Not the president. Mike knew the president already had bodyguards that had been in place for a while. Mike wasn't sure he would want that responsibility anyway.

"Mr. President, Captain Calloway is here," the President's Chief of Staff, Paul Romero, announced. Romero looked the part. He was not so large as to be intimidating but the perfectly cut suit couldn't hide the muscular body underneath. Most would think twice before they confronted him. He oozed competence and affability. Mike noticed how well the man carried himself. *He's had martial arts training, a lot of training.*

"Send him in, Paul."

"Sir." Mike snapped off his best salute and stood at attention until President Harris told him to relax and have a seat in front of the huge Oval Office desk. Mike sat down and tried his best not to fidget. He was nervous. After all, this was the president of the United States. This was the Office of the President where world-changing decisions were made.

President Harris looked closely at the young man in front of him. Something was odd. After a couple of minutes, he could tell his scrutiny was making the young man begin to fidget. Not much, just a little. He couldn't put his finger on what was bothering him.

"Do you want this job, son?"

"I...I...don't know sir. It's kind of out of my usual range of assignments."

"Yes, well, I was told of the need for a little easier workload for you. You've made quite a name for yourself at a very young age, Captain Calloway...Mike. May I call you Mike?"

"Yes, of course, sir."

"How much do you know of my family, Mike?"

"Not a lot, sir, just what everyone else knows, maybe not even that much. I was out of the country during most of your term." Mike wasn't sure exactly how much the president wanted from him.

"Okay. Then I'll give you just a little run down. Most of it you will probably know. Did you know I wanted to be president when I was eight years old?"

"Ah...no."

"Well, I did. I decided that would be my goal. And I have worked for that goal my whole life. Not because of the fame or the power, believe it or not. I felt I had something to contribute, an ideal I thought America needed. It's not been as easy to promote that ideal as I had hoped. But it's still there. My family has been through a lot, more than I should ever have asked of them. But they have always been my main support. With God in the center of our family, we have weathered everything outside forces have thrown at us."

Mike had relaxed as the president was speaking. He had heard of the president's strong faith. He just didn't know how vocal he was about it.

The president continued to watch Mike as he spoke. "There have been other bodyguards during the last three plus years, of course, and a couple have been really bad choices. I take responsibility for those. I should have met them before they were assigned, but I didn't. I accepted them at someone else's urging. I won't make that mistake again. Do you have any questions so far?"

"I know I'm supposed to be assigned to one of your daughters, but I wasn't told which one."

"Ah, yes. Well, as you may be aware, I have four daughters. Madeline is our oldest daughter. She is a pediatrician and she has her own place. Dolly is the next oldest. She's married and has a house in Virginia. She's an artist and her husband, Louis, is also an artist with his own studio. DeeAnn lives here and is in her second year of college. My youngest daughter is Brooke. That's where the problem is going to be."

"Problem, sir?"

"Ahem. Yes. My youngest daughter is seventeen. She is very...how shall I put this? Strong willed? She doesn't want a bodyguard."

"But she has to have one."

"Yes, absolutely. She just will not give in to that fact. And...because of her attitude, we've gone through several bodyguards over the years. She can be quite creative in her protest."

"So, anyone guarding her would have to be very vigilant. And ready for any kind of retaliation?"

"I see. You understand perfectly. Do you think you could be that person?"

"Maybe." Mike didn't have a clue why he said that. He didn't need the headache. He wanted to get back in shape and go back to being a soldier.

"Come back tomorrow and meet the family. I have a feeling this will work out." He shook Mike's hand and called for his Chief-of-Staff to show Mike out.

CHAPTER 19

It made him smile that he was using the information he had gotten from Randi during the tour. He made his way to the family area without any trouble. Guards at each point checked off his name on their lists. No one got by without being on the lists. Finally standing in front of the last set of doors, Mike went in as soon as the guard opened the door and waved him in.

"Why do I have to have a bodyguard? I'm seventeen. I can take care of myself. What about the last two? They were such losers! I can't put up with more of the same thing."

"Honey, settle down, please." Mike gazed at the scene in front of him, taking in each person. As he stepped forward, they all turned to look at him. He felt like a bug under a microscope. President Harris was trying to soothe his youngest daughter, but it didn't seem to be helping much. The other three daughters were sitting silently on the long sofa. All three were very pretty. Make that four. Even the youngest daughter had a fresh, natural beauty, even though at the moment she had a scowl on her face.

"We are so sorry." The president's wife walked toward him with her hand extended. "Thank you for coming. Please, can I get you something to drink…a cola, water?"

He shook her hand and said, "No, thank you. I'm fine." The moment their hands touched, Mike felt the strangest sensation. He wanted to pull this woman, the wife of the President of the United States, into his arms and crush her in a hug! Of course he would never do such a thing.

"Is something wrong, Captain Calloway?"

"No, ma'am. Just nervous, I guess."

Celeste Harris was still a beauty. Eyes a cerulean blue, hair light brown with very little gray mixed in. When she smiled at him, he felt drawn to her.

"Well, let's just talk a little. Get acquainted. We'll get to the other stuff later, okay?" As Celeste let go of the young man's hand she had the strangest sensation that she had held his hand before.

"Have we ever met before, Captain Calloway?"

"I…don't believe so, ma'am."

She shook her head slightly, smiled and motioned for him to have a seat.

The President had to leave, saying he had a meeting he just couldn't put off.

Celeste and Mike talked for well over an hour about general things, the economy, foreign affairs, his view on politics. Prompted by Celeste's gentle questioning, he opened up about his faith and moral values. The four girls had to leave for an appointment, but Mike and the First Lady continued to discuss duties and restrictions.

"Oh, my. Where has the time gone? I guess we better get down to the business part. My husband will request your transfer as soon as the background check has been completed. That is if you agree to take on this mission, and I'm afraid that is what it's going to be. My youngest daughter can be quite a handful. She had a bad experience with the last couple of bodyguards." She sighed. "We all did."

His head felt like it was whirling around. Did he want to tackle this? For some reason he heard himself say, "Yes. I would like to have the position and I will do my best to change your family's opinion of bodyguards."

"I have a feeling you will, Mike." She reached over and squeezed his hand, which for some weird reason made him want to cry. When he glanced up he saw the same emotion in her eyes.

Mike trailed Brooke, the President's youngest daughter, while she tried on dress after dress at the fancy boutique. She had been very vocal about not wanting a bodyguard, but finally accepted that it was going to happen anyway. She had no choice. Still, she was determined to make his life as miserable as possible. *Why had he said he would take this on?*

"What about this one?" she asked for the umpteenth time. The party was this weekend and she had yet to find a dress that suited her. All her friends had their dresses. Of course, they could choose whatever they wanted. Brooke had to be careful in her choice. It has to pass her Mother's okay as well as the White House aides that governed what the President's wife and children wore to public functions. It was a big concession that she was allowed to shop for her own dress. The press would have a field day if it didn't look just right.

She really didn't care what he thought. She just wanted to get to him. Make him look foolish. It was something she was good at. In the week he had been watching over her, she had taken every opportunity to berate and embarrass him.

He had tried to take it in stride, but it was really getting to him. No one should treat another person that way.

God, I'm going to need your help on this one. Help me have the right attitude. Help me say the right words to help Brooke. Something has hurt or scared her, and I don't know what it is.

"The color's not right."

"What? Of course it is. I love red."

She hadn't expected him to answer. This was a first. Maybe she was finally getting to him. It had taken a lot longer than she had envisioned.

"It's just not a good color for you."

Now she was curious. "Why?"

"Why what?" She sounded angry. *Was she mad that he talked back to her or because he didn't think she looked good in red?*

She thought for a moment. *What was it about this guy? She just couldn't get a fix on what made him tick.* She'd tried everything she could think of. Browbeating, embarrassment…nothing seemed to get to him.

True, he had been a perfect gentleman, not like some she had known. *Maybe, just maybe...she would be okay with Mike. He was definitely good looking. She had seen how all the women in the boutique were swooning over him. And he had perfect manners and...wait, wait. Wasn't she trying to get rid of the bodyguard? Instead, here she was almost swooning herself! Ugh!*

"Why not red?"

"Because..."

"What? Were you just trying to get at me?" Now she was getting angry. *How dare he...*

"No. Okay. This is just my humble opinion...being a man...but the color is too much. I just see a red dress. Not you."

She thought that over for a moment. Turning to the mirror, she held the dress in front of herself. It was a beautiful dress, the red so vivid. Everyone would see her coming a mile away. Was that what she wanted? No! She didn't want to look like a beacon. She wanted a dress that said, "Wow, there's Brooke. She looks great," and *then*, "What is that she's wearing? It looks fantastic on her."

"Oh...I never thought of it that way." She hesitated. "Pick one out."

Oh no. What have I done?

She couldn't believe she had said that. What in the world? Well, she didn't have to get whatever he picked out. She could make fun of his choice and go ahead and get the red dress or find one at another store. With that decided she put her hands on her hips and glared at him.

"Go ahead, make a choice. There are plenty to choose from."

He knew a challenge when he heard one. "Okay." He gave her a little smile as he turned away.

While the other bodyguards watched at the door, Mike walked around the fancy boutique not finding anything he felt she wouldn't reject at first sight. Finally drifting into another room he found what he considered a beautiful dress for Brooke. It was a shimmery pale blue. Not cut too low for a young girl, but trendy and sleek. If he was picking something out for one of his sisters, he would think it perfect for her. Of course, he wasn't going to tell Princess Brooke that.

He picked up a long pink dress with many ruffles and placed it in front of the pale blue one. He had a hard time keeping a straight face as he approached her in the other room.

"Ha! I didn't figure you would come up with anything. I wouldn't be caught dead in that dress. It's awful!! How old do you think I am? Ten?"

"It's a very nice dress. Nice price, too." When he saw the ticket on the dress, he almost passed out.

"Your taste in clothes is horrendous. Never mind. We'll go to another store. I'm not finding anything here."

He kept his face as neutral as possible as he took the dress in his other arm to put it away. That uncovered the blue dress so Brooke could see it.

"Wait." He had turned to go to the other room, but turned back as Brooke came toward him. "What is that?" pointing at the shimmery dress in his other hand.

"Oh, I must have accidentally picked this up behind the other one. Let me put these back up and we'll move on to the next store. It's getting pretty late. You have to be back by five, remember."

"Yeah. I remember. Hey, let me see that blue one. I like the material."

A little smile played around Mike's lips as Brooke took the gown into the dressing room to try on. He turned toward the bodyguard at the door and caught his eyes watching him. Mike nodded to him and the guy gave him a little salute. He had caught on to Mike's ploy. Mike just hoped Brooke didn't.

CHAPTER 20

The party was in full swing. Mike still wasn't sure what the party was for, but there were a lot of young people, and many of them were on the dance floor. Brooke looked like she was having fun being the center of attention. She swirled by in her sparkling blue dress and gave a little wave. Mike smiled. Brooke had lightened up some after their shopping trip. He just hoped it wasn't a ruse to get him to let his guard down.

"What are you doing here?"

Mike whirled around and there was Randi! Of all people, he hadn't expected to meet her here. Though it would stand to reason that she would be invited. She and the President's daughters were probably friends, especially since she worked in the White House as tour guide. He realized he had been staring at her for quite a while and hadn't even said hello.

"Hi," was all he could squeeze past the lump that had caught in his throat. Randi looked quite incredible. The black dress she wore was of some soft clingy material that shimmered in the lights from the chandeliers. She was…

Brooke breezed by, "Oh! Randi. You look fantastic. By the way, meet Mike, my new bodyguard."

"New bodyguard, huh?"

"Uh, yeah."

Randi waved a hand in front of his face, "Are you okay there?" You look a little out of it? You haven't been drinking have you?" Her voice had sharpened.

"I'm alright. And no, I haven't been drinking. I happen to be on duty."

She stared at him for another minute before turning around and walking off.

Okay…that was weird. What is it with her?

"Mike!" Mike turned around and saw Jeff and Will. They were both dressed nicer than he had ever seen them. Will had on jeans and a dark sports coat with a white shirt, while Jeff actually had on a nice dark suit with a grey shirt and striped tie.

"Hey, you know Randi?"

Mike could sense the disapproval in Jeff's voice. Maybe he was Randi's boyfriend. "We just met at one of the White House tours."

"Oh. Okay. Just don't get any ideas about our sister. She doesn't like men in uniform."

Sister! And he had rented a room from her brothers. How lucky could one man be?

How unlucky can one girl get? The man from the tour was right here in D.C. and a bodyguard for President Harris's daughter, Brooke. She had felt like a schoolgirl that day at the White House. Her pulse had raced and she couldn't put a decent sentence together. It was those blue, blue eyes. Trouble, that's what he was. She knew without a doubt that he was going to disturb her well-ordered life. She wanted to work for the White House long enough to learn as much as she could about how things worked in government. Eventually she wanted to be an ambassador, like her dad. If she had a choice, she would like to be ambassador to Israel. She had even been working on getting the language down.

CHAPTER 21

"This race is going to be a tough one. You know Hadley will pull every trick in the book. He wants my job in the worst way." Cole Harris paced around the Oval Office with his Vice-President, Mel Myers, following him with his eyes.

Myers was the perfect Vice-President. His physical attributes and polished speech may have helped to get him elected, but Cole treasured his levelheaded advice. He was also a good friend. He had worked his way up the ladder in almost the same way Cole had. Police force, then district attorney. Cole went on to be governor, and Mel became a State Attorney General. Cole thought he would make an excellent president some day soon.

"Cole, we're ahead by double digits. You are going to be President for a second term. Horace Hadley doesn't have what it takes. Besides that, he's a crook. His last Senatorial race was as dirty as it gets."

Cole walked over to the window to look out over the back garden. It was so nice this time of year. Everything green with bursts of colorful flowers and shrubs. Did he even want a second term? He was tired. No…he couldn't let Hadley win…for the good of the country. He just dreaded what kind of smear campaign Horace Hadley was going to come up with against him and his family. He knew Horace well. Had known him for over twenty years. Knew he was not beyond manufacturing any kind of smut against him or, God forbid, his family.

"Haven't you come up with anything? Time is running out and I need something, anything…even if it's not true. As long as it can create a question to Harris's character."

"Horace, I've searched and searched. He's so clean he squeaks when he walks." Bob Meeker, Horace's campaign manager flung himself onto the overstuffed sofa. "Other than inventing something…"

There was a deathly silence in the room. *Meeker won't want to do it,* but, Horace sneered to himself, *he'll do it. He has to. His love of his wife's money will insure that.* Hadley could end Meeker's marriage to his wealthy wife with the little piece of paper he had in his pocket.

"Like what? I mean it would have to be very subtle…and not traceable to me."

"Wait…wait…I don't know about this. I mean, well, Harris is very popular with the people. It could end up backfiring on us. Couldn't we pound him on the issues?"

"I need to have an edge. I don't have that right now. Find something, or find yourself another job!" Hadley glared at his campaign manager as if it was his fault that everything wasn't going the way Horace wanted it to.

That had been Horace's problem all his life. If things weren't going right, it must be someone else's fault. He blamed his parents for not having enough money to send him to the best schools. He blamed his teachers for his grades not being high enough to get the scholarships he wanted. He blamed his wife for him not being in the social circle he wanted. Soon enough, however, he would have everything he wanted, the power, hobnobbing with the elite, and fame. His picture would be on the wall of the White House forever.

CHAPTER 22

Randi was sorry she had been so short with Brooke's new bodyguard. He seemed kind of nice. Of course, looks can be deceiving. That she was even worrying about what he thought surprised her. What surprised her even more was how her heart rate picked up and she felt her cheeks flush when he turned those incredible blue eyes on her, just like it had the first time when she had met him on the tour. *What was his name? Mike?* She shook her head at her own musings. No way. He was a heartache just waiting to happen, and she didn't need any more problems.

She had her life mapped out and it didn't include a military man who might go off and get himself killed leaving her with children to bring up on her own. She had seen that happen to two of her friends from high school. Both of them were having a hard time coping. Sally had it extra hard because the bills just kept piling up and her little two-year-old son had some health problems. Her husband had only been in the army for six months when the transport vehicle he was riding in was hit with an IED, an improvised explosive device.

Three men had lost their lives. Three men who would not come home to their families.

Devon's husband never saw his little daughter. He was killed three months before Holly was born. He was a Navy SEAL. They had an operation go bad and several men were hurt. Only Tad was killed.

The only thing they ever said to Randi was that they were proud of their husbands' service for their country.

CHAPTER 23

Mel faced his friend. "Cole, I don't know how they dug up this information. They probably went back to where you were living at the time. But it…it's ridiculous. What can they make out of it? Your son disappeared. You and Celeste were cleared of any suspicion. You spent, what, almost fifty thousand dollars searching for him. They never found any clues other than a few drops of blood. No one saw anything, knew anything. Nothing."

Cole looked at his second-in-command and friend. "They don't have to make anything of it. All they have to do is insinuate and whisper suspicions. The press will do the rest. They will have me crucified without a shred of evidence." He pressed his fingers to his tired eyes. They were in the Oval Office, had been since early morning, going over the budget, problems with Iran, and now this crazy thing Hadley had initiated. Everyone knew it was Hadley, or someone in his party, who brought up the question of Cole's missing son.

"I don't care for my sake or for the campaign. My family will be drug through this again, reminded of all we went through, reminded of our loss." His voice broke on the last word. Just thinking about his son was more than he could stand. It had been so many years and not a word. They had given up. Had to. He was gone, possibly…probably dead. He wiped his eyes with the back of his hand.

"Get something together. We have to nip this before it gets going. Put the information out there." Mel couldn't believe what he was hearing.

"Cole! No…no, that would be suicide. Why would you want to do that?"

The idea was beginning to take root in Cole's mind. It just might work. Take the wind out of Hadley's sails. And just maybe…maybe someone will come forward with some information about Sean. His beautiful son. He still missed him…every day. He wondered what his son would have looked like. He remembered the little boy he had been. Built much like his daddy, he was tall for his twelve years. He would be a pretty big man. Slender? Maybe. He had had light blonde hair like Celeste's, had her blue eyes. Cole felt his control slipping and had to rein in his emotions. He had to do something.

"Fix up a report. We will tell the people about Sean, how he disappeared off the face of the earth. How we've never given up hope." Even though they had. "Make a plea for help. Any information. Maybe someone will come forward."

"Cole, Cole. Can your family survive that?" Mel grieved for his friend. The look in Cole's eyes said it all. He would not let this go now that he had made the decision. It was obvious he had never given up hope that his son was still alive…somewhere.

"Alright, Cole. I'll have it fixed up by this evening. I just hope you're not making a big mistake."

It was a mistake. Cole didn't realize what a big one it was going to be. He should never have come out with the information. But he had to do something. It was an area of his life he had not shared with the public, and Hadley could certainly use it against him. Make him look suspect.

Bringing the information out had taken any power for Hadley to use it against him, but now it was becoming a circus, with young men coming out of the woodwork claiming to be his long lost son. He should have figured that. Some of course were quickly weeded out. A few would have to submit DNA samples. Phone calls were screened and very few gave any hope of information. It didn't matter. Cole knew he would have done the same thing over again. If there was even one chance in a billion that his son could be found, alive or dead, it was worth it.

One good thing that came out of it was that Horace Hadley had been outmaneuvered. Not one peep since they had come out with the plea. Cole could just imagine Hadley's face when he read the report. He might laugh at the media circus, but he would also see that his ploy had been scotched.

Mike had listened to Brooke and her sisters as they railed against the men trying to get to the President through them. One had even bumped Madeline's car just so he could talk to her. Of course the young man didn't get very far with her bodyguard there. Checking his background revealed several outstanding tickets, so he was in even more trouble. "Why in the world did Daddy do this? It's horrible!" DeeAnn railed, "I don't want to relive all of it again. Sean has to be dead or…or we would have heard from him. Wouldn't we?"

DeeAnn looked over to where Mike was standing guard at the door of the exclusive salon. "Wouldn't someone have contacted us for money if Sean had been still alive?"

"Sean?" Mike asked with a frown of incomprehension.

"Our brother. He had just turned twelve. Got a camera for his birthday." Madeline, who was eight years older, could remember how excited Sean was. "He just had to go out that evening to take pictures with his new camera. We never heard from him again." Her voice broke on the last word. Since she was so much older than Sean, she could remember more about him. At times he had been the typical younger brother, but at other times he was the sweetest, most gallant little boy Madeline had ever seen. He looked after his family of girls when their dad had to be away for meetings. He was so smart in school. He had even helped Madeline with some of her math and she was way ahead of him in school. In some ways Mike reminded her of Sean.

It made it hard for Madeline to be very friendly with Mike, for some reason. Sean would have been a few years younger than Mike though.

"I'm so sorry." Mike couldn't imagine their pain. The not knowing.

"Let's get out of here. I don't want to do this any-more." Dolly could remember so little about Sean and it bothered her. It was like she had abandoned his memory. She was fourteen when he disappeared. Surely she should remember more about her only brother. She picked up her things and headed out the door to the limousine assigned to them. Brooke followed her sisters out of the salon with a pensive look on her face. She had few memories of her older brother. It was like he had faded out of existence.

CHAPTER 24

Jeff and Will were at the apartment when Mike got home. They had pots on the stove and some wonderful smells were permeating the room. "Wow, that smells great."

"Thanks, would you like some?"

"No, no I…"

"Hey, there's plenty. Come on join us." Will pulled another plate from the cabinet and set it in front of Mike. The plate was plain white with a little chip out of the corner, but it matched the other two plates in the set. The chips were just in a different place on each.

"Sorry about the plates. Some of the young guys are a little hard on our fine china when they help wash up," Jeff said with a rueful smile.

Mike filled his plate and sat at the table with Jeff and Will. All three young men automatically bowed their heads. Jeff led in a prayer of thanks for their food, for their family and friends, and for Jesus who died on the cross for them. They raised their heads, looked at each other, and said "amen" at the same time. For the first time in a long while, Mike felt like part of a family. He had just forgotten that the family of God was everywhere.

The spaghetti was delicious and the conversation was even better. Will had to give the devotion at the next youth meeting and he went over some of the things he had been studying. Jeff asked him to clarify a couple of points and Mike pulled out his Bible to read over the verses. The verses really spoke to his heart.

As he got ready for bed, Mike went over things in his mind. He sat down on his bed and propped his back against the headboard, going over everything the girls said earlier that day. There was something bothering him. He just couldn't get a handle on it. Sure, the girls had been upset, but he didn't know them well enough to be that affected by their sorrow. Still, his heart hurt for them, for the pain they were going through. "Sean. Sean Harris. Forever twelve years old. How sad." He prayed for the girls and for the President and First Lady. For Sean, if he was still alive.

Waking up in a cold sweat after a restless night's sleep, Mike couldn't figure out what had him so on edge. His last thought before waking was that someone was after him. He felt like he had run a marathon. If Brooke was in one of her moods, it was going to be a rough day. He hoped not. He wasn't in the mood to put up with her antics.

What had he heard right before he woke up? A man's voice yelling at him…but he couldn't make out what he was saying, just that he was very angry. He was chasing him, and Mike couldn't get far enough away. His legs felt like they were in quicksand, and it was slowing him down. All of a sudden there was a flash and a terrible pain in his head. That's when he woke up. He couldn't figure out if it was just a dream, make that *nightmare*, or if it was a memory trying to break through. If it was a memory, who could the man have been?

CHAPTER 25

Horace Hadley was in a panic. He didn't know what to do about this situation. He went over what Harris had pulled out of his box of tricks. It was in all the papers, on the television, even You-Tube.

"Twelve year old, camera, disappeared. Why did it never occur to me? Stupid. Stupid! That boy, all those years ago. He was Cole's son. That little stinking rat that took my picture. Why was he out there anyway? It was dark. Wasn't he too young to be out in that part of the city by himself?"

He walked over behind his desk and threw himself into the chair. "I hope no one comes forward. Please, please don't let anyone come forward with information. I just wanted to make trouble for Harris in order to help my lagging campaign. I can't afford to have any one show up with information now." He pulled at his tie, loosening the knot so he could breathe better. The tie felt like a noose around his neck. He had to find that boy if he was still alive. If he was dead, as Hadley hoped, then he was home free. He just couldn't take that chance.

"You! Keep an eye on this situation, take care of it." When he pointed a long finger toward Bob Meeker, he noticed his hand was shaking. He pulled his hand back down under his desk, but not before Meeker saw it.

"Me? This is your problem. I wasn't even there ten years ago." Meeker glared at his employer. He wasn't doing any more for this man. Hadley was nervous and that wasn't a good sign. He could just as easily turn on Meeker and set him up to take the fall for whatever was done.

"You're my campaign manager. And really, Bob, what's a little more graft and corruption between friends. Remember, you've been there all the way with me."

Bob Meeker's throat squeezed shut at Hadley's tone. "Yeah…I remember. I'll do what I can." *Pitiful,* he thought. *I'm a pitiful excuse for a man.*

Horace grabbed his arm as he turned away. "Find out if there is anything…anything about that boy after that night. I know I hit him. His blood was found on some rocks near where I shot. He should be dead, but if he's not, make him that way. Got it?"

Bob nodded and slipped out the door. He was shaking so hard he could hardly walk. This was getting out of hand. He was tired of doing Hadley's dirty work, but he didn't have much choice. He had made his bed with the devil and he couldn't get out of it now. Where had he gone so wrong?

CHAPTER 26

Mike was up earlier than usual. Something about his dreams just kept interrupting his sleep. He figured since he was already awake he may as well go for a run. He thought about asking Jeff and Will if they would like to join him, but they were still in bed. He had no idea when they came in to go to bed. It must have been after midnight. What did they do that kept them out so late? Party? Or work? He'd have to ask them what jobs they had. He didn't think they were into anything shady, but he didn't want to keep assuming. Better to just come out and ask.

He opened the door and stepped out...straight into Randi's arms.

"Oh! Sorry...I didn't expect anyone to be there."

Randi had to clear the knot out of her throat before she could squeak out an answer. "It's okay, ahem, I just...I came to see if my brothers would join me in a run." She was having a hard time getting out a decent sentence since Mike still had his arms around her waist. She could feel the hard muscle of his arms and smell the clean scent of his aftershave. It did strange things to her heart rate. She stepped back a little and Mike let his arms fall to his sides. He had on his standard running shorts with a Marines tee shirt that showed off his toned abs and muscled arms.

"I think they got in pretty late. They were still dead to the world." He was taking in the sight of her. She had on a pair of lemon yellow running shorts and a darker yellow sleeveless top. With her hair up in a ponytail, she looked gorgeous. But she also looked about fourteen.

"Oh, okay. I'll just…"

"Would you mind if I joined you? I was just headed out anyway. You could show me the best routes to run."

After a long pause Randi seemed to make up her mind, "I guess I could give you the official running tour."

"Official, huh?"

"Yep! Given to all newbies."

With a lightness in his step that wasn't there a few minutes before, he followed Randi's lead through the runners' paths that wound around the area. It was a perfect day for running, a little cool, but not cold. The air was crisp and surprisingly fresh this close in to the city.

His side was beginning to twinge by the time Randi relented and slowed down to a more comfortable pace. Randi must have seen him reach for his side because she slowed down even more.

"Sorry, I tend to run pretty much flat out. I guess I thought you were in a lot better shape. To get a body like that…" She shut her mouth on a gasp and blushed all the way to the tips of her ears. *How could she have said something like that?*

He saw her delightful blush and thought about teasing her, but he didn't want to embarrass her any more, so he pretended he didn't hear. He didn't correct her impression of his ability, either. She didn't need to know all the history behind his pain. He stooped down with the excuse he needed to tighten his shoelace, and gave her time for her face to cool down.

They walked for a little ways making light conversation. It was surprising to Randi how much they had to talk about. She really enjoyed the continuous banter back and forth, some of it teasing, some serious topics as well. After a while, they both agreed they were ready to finish up with a run back to the apartment. Randi laughed when they pulled up side by side. She was puffing by that time. She noticed Mike wasn't even out of breath, but he was holding his side again. She wanted to ask if he was okay, but she didn't know if that was too personal a question and she had already embarrassed herself once today. When he turned those gorgeous eyes on her she tended to get flustered and her brain turned to mush.

"That was a great run. Thanks for giving me the *official* tour." Mike had grabbed her hand in his and was smiling down at her. She felt the heat from his palm sizzling up her arm like an electrical current. It made her jump a little and pull her hand away quickly. To hide her reaction she turned and started jogging away, giving a little wave over her shoulder. "You're welcome. Keep practicing. Maybe you'll be able to keep up with me next time!" she smiled to take any sting out of what she said.

"*Next time,*" *she said.* That made Mike smile. There might be a next time in the future. He watched her jog away and his heart felt light and fluttery.

CHAPTER 27

"Darling, I think we have a big mess." Celeste looked over at her husband. He was bent over his desk going over all the memos and papers that had been brought to his attention. He raised his head enough to look at his wife. She was still the most beautiful woman he had ever seen, inside and out. He hated bringing all this back into their lives. They had dealt with what happened with their son in the only way they could. They had pushed it away to the far recesses of their hearts. They still loved Sean, but they couldn't think of him every day and remain able to function.

For months after Sean's disappearance, Celeste had battled with depression. She felt she should have done more to protect her son. She had bought Sean the camera. Maybe if she hadn't he wouldn't have gone out that night. She would wake up at night crying and it began to affect her care of their daughters. Their pastor had suggested a good Christian counselor that could help not only Celeste but the whole family. Cole didn't realize how much the loss had affected his daughters as well as himself. He thought he had dealt with it. He found that he had pushed it down deep, buried it along with part of his heart.

"Yes, babe. I really did it this time. I'm so sorry." Celeste got up and knelt in front of him. Laying her head on his arm, she sighed. So many young men had tried to pass themselves off as the president's son. When the media put their story out there, many men between the ages of eighteen to forty had claimed to be their long lost son, thinking to gain fame or money. *Why couldn't one of them be Sean? Was it possible he was still alive?*

"We will get through this, with God's help, just like we always have. Maybe we'll even find some new information." She knew it was a long shot, but, like Cole, if there were any chance at all, she would have taken it, too.

"I love you. You know that, don't you?" He pulled her head toward his just as the door opened and all four of their daughters piled into the room.

"Dad…Mom…" all four girls started talking at once.

"Hi, girls. Whatcha need?" Cole gazed at their beautiful daughters, their family. He loved them more than life itself. He and Celeste were so blessed. If only…

"Hey, Mike, not working today?" Will looked at him over his very large glass of orange juice.

Mike was usually up and out of the apartment long before the two brothers were even awake. He still woke up as early as usual but he had taken his time getting ready for the day. Studying his Bible and spending extra long over his quiet time had put him in an excellent mood.

"Not today."

"How come?" Jeff poked his brother in the arm.

"That's not your business, bro." The two men were dressed in similar clothing, loose, slightly faded jeans with long sleeved pullover shirts. The shirts had their names on the front and the name of their church on the back. They appeared to be headed out for the day.

"It's okay. No big secret. Brooke is grounded for the day for some reason. So I get the day off." He pulled a bowl and a box of cereal out of the cabinet.

Will smiled and slapped Mike on the back hard enough to dislocate something.

"Great! How about you come and help us out today?"

"Will…" Jeff groaned, "Mike just said he had the day off. He doesn't want to fill it working with us. I'm sure he has all kinds of plans, maybe a girlfriend to see."

Will looked so crestfallen Mike couldn't help but ask, "Work? I didn't know you two worked."

Will spluttered, "Well, of course we work. How would we be able to pay our share of the rent on this place? I'm wounded, Mike." Then, he looked at the teasing light in Mike's face. "Aw, man, you got me."

"What kind of work do you two do?"

Jeff reached over and grabbed his brother by the neck in a loose chokehold.

"This young man is a computer doc. You have a problem with your computer, call him and he can get you fixed right up. Even big companies with networks call him all the time. He just logs his hours and leaves them a bill when he's through. He can fix anything." It was obvious that Jeff was very proud of his little brother.

Will wiggled out of the chokehold and poked Jeff hard in the ribs.

"Jeff is the youth director at our church. He is great with the kids, and they really respect him. He also does some volunteer work, like today."

Mike's raised eyebrows asked the question for him.

"Oh, you know… soup kitchen, mowing yards for a couple of older people in our church, that sort of thing." The guys actually looked embarrassed.

"I think it's wonderful that you two are willing to do those things for people in need. I can think of nothing I'd rather do than to help you out today. Just let me grab a bite to eat and I'll be ready." He grabbed the milk out of the refrigerator and poured some over his cereal.

"You sure? No girlfriend to see?" Mike knew Will was just fishing for information, but he just shrugged his shoulders and began to eat his cereal. He didn't know why a young woman with pale blonde hair and startling blue eyes came to his mind. It made him smile, and Will and Jeff looked at each other knowingly.

"Well, what have you got? It's been over two weeks." Hadley paced back and forth across his office floor. He scowled at his campaign manager.

"I know, Horace, but you're asking the almost impossible," Bob growled in response." You know how slow these things can be, especially if you don't want just anyone knowing what you're digging into. I've had to cover and at times pay under the table for a little extra effort." He held up his hand when Horace would have asked again. "Yes, now…it's not much but I think I'm on to something. You remember the blood the cops found?" At his nod, Bob went on. "I've got the best DNA experts and computer nerds that money, *your* money, can buy looking for a match. If he's still alive and has ever had blood drawn for DNA analysis we'll find it, and him."

"If he's had blood drawn for that." He gave a skeptical glance at Meeker.

"Yeah, well like I said, it's an almost impossible task."

"What if he's not alive?" Hadley rubbed at a patch of whiskers he had missed when he shaved that morning. He really needed to pay more attention to his looks. After all, he was going to be President. He needed to have a good personal image.

"Well, then your troubles would be over, wouldn't they?" Hadley murmured an agreement, but he had a bad feeling about the situation.

Horace Hadley gawked at his campaign manager. "You…you actually found him? Alive?" All the blood seemed to drain out of his head, leaving him feeling dizzy. *Alive. No, no, no, this can't happen now.* Not when he was beginning to gain a little in the polls. He wanted to be president, wanted the power and prestige.

Of course, he also wanted the lasting benefits. Even after he was no longer in office he would be sought out for seminars and asked his opinion on things. He could write books and they would sell just because of who he was.

"Yes, alive and well and living here in Washington. He had offered to be a bone marrow donor for a fellow marine who had developed leukemia. That database was the perfect place to check. I can tell you it took some finagling to get that information. It was quite expensive for *you*." Bob had an almost gleeful expression on his face. He didn't mind seeing Hadley squirm a bit. He hated being under Hadley's thumb all the time. He was trying to keep his voice down since the restaurant they were in was almost full, but it was hard to hear across the large table and he didn't want to move to a seat closer to Hadley.

"Bob, you know what needs to be done. Get...it... done, now." He emphasized each word. Noting the reluctance forming on Bob's face, Hadley pulled a little note from his vest pocket. He didn't even have to read it to Bob. Bob knew what it was, and his color turned a sickly grey.

Bob nodded his head once, showing that he understood the threat. He had no choice. What was on that sheet of paper...his life would be ruined, his wife...and her money...gone. He didn't mind so much about his wife, but the money... that was a different story.

CHAPTER 28

Mike had thoroughly enjoyed the day that he worked with Jeff and Will. He really liked working with them, and he liked the fact that he was helping others. He hadn't done much of that since his parents had been killed. When he was first with the couple that took him in, he found out very quickly how much they did for others. They were generous givers in their church, but they went beyond that to others in need. They showed Mike how it benefitted not just the person helped, but it was such a blessing for the giver.

It was an added bonus that he got to work beside Randi. She was beginning to loosen up a bit toward him. Even teased him some. He wanted to ask her out, but he didn't think she was ready to go that far yet. He watched her when she wasn't looking. She had an easy manner with people. Her kind heart showed through in everything she did. Sometimes he would catch a sad look in her eyes and he wondered what caused it. He finally asked her about it. She just shook her head.

"It's so sad that as much as we try to help, there are so many people in need that you can't help them all."

Mike worked all day at the soup kitchen helping to prepare the food and then serving the meals. Later on in the day he went with Jeff and Will, reluctantly leaving Randi to clean up the kitchen. Not that he liked washing dishes, especially the pots and pans, but he hated to leave Randi.

The guys had made plans to clean up two yards, mowing down some tall grass that had died in the early winter chill, and getting rid of piles of fallen leaves. They needed Mike's help because the yards were huge and they needed to finish them today. Tomorrow they had other tasks they had taken on. The men took to their tasks with gusto, Mike right along side of them and barely finished before it got too dark to see what they were doing.

Even in their fun and games Mike could tell that the boys really cared for each other and for their sister. He could imagine what it was like when Randi and all her brothers were together in one house. It must have been fun growing up with brothers and sisters. He wanted his kids to have that some day. When he found the right girl to marry. God had that planned. He knew that, but he sure wouldn't mind having at least a clue. He thought of the girl working beside him in the soup line earlier and thought, *Maybe...?*

Mike was settling in well in the apartment. Jeff and Will were great guys. When they had the youth over for Bible study and food, Mike would usually join them. He could carry his own in the discussion and sometimes he felt he could actually connect a little better with a couple of the hesitant youth. He knew what it was like to feel alone and afraid but not have anyone to talk to about it. If he could just get them to see that God was always there, ready to listen even if no one else would.

Mike had brought all his things to the apartment from the one where he was staying in California. He had gotten rid of much of it at the local homeless shelter, but he had some personal things and a few things of his parents' he couldn't bear to part with. It had involved getting off from his job for a few days, since he had to drive to Pasadena, as well. He didn't want to leave those strange pictures that far away. Why that bothered him he just didn't know. He just knew he wanted them close by. When he got back to D.C. he found a bank within an hour's drive and put the pictures in a safety deposit box there. He didn't want the pictures in a bank too close to him. He wasn't sure why. He just felt the need to have a little space between him and the photos. He also left his will in the box. He had no relatives that he knew of, so he had to make provisions for all the money he had. Money from the house in California that he was renting to a very nice family. He just couldn't part with the house. There were too many memories. They were the only memories he had of family. There was the money from his parents' estate, insurance money, money that had accumulated from his salary. He used so little of it that it just kept adding up in his bank account. He just didn't need that much to live on. He left a letter with the bank president to be opened in case something happened to him.

CHAPTER 29

"Please, Mom, please. I promise I won't ask another thing in like...forever." Brooke was trying to wheedle her mother into letting her go to a concert with some of her friends from school. The Harris girls had all gone to a private Christian school that also had other girls from wealthy and or influential families. The security at the school had been beefed up even more when Cole Harris had become president. Brooke really liked the school and loved all the friends she had made, but it was very strict.

"Brooke, darling, you have to understand how much this one outing would cost in money and manpower. Just because we can use bodyguards and extra pre-cautions and scanners, all those things that go into keeping you safe, doesn't mean that it's right to abuse those things. We have an obligation to the people of the United States to use this office and the money it takes to run it and the country with care. We have to remember that each person in America who pays taxes, whether income tax or sales tax, are *our* bosses. Use their money wisely for the good of the country."

Brooke understood, she really did. But still it hurt not to be able to do things the other girls did. She slunk off to her room and stayed there even through dinner.

Of course she had her own money, money her grandparents had left her and each of her sisters, but she couldn't touch that until she was twenty-one. She didn't know if she even wanted to touch it then. It was so sad, her mother's parents dying of cancer within three weeks of each other. Her granddad had lung cancer and her grandmother had had a long battle with breast cancer that was caught too late. Even if she could, she would never use that money on something so trivial as a concert. Trivial, that was just what it was! Why was she in her room moping? She shook her head at her own silliness. That concert didn't mean that much. She went to her parents' suite and hugged her mom. She inhaled the scent of her mother, the perfume she always wore. That smell would be forever etched in her memory.

"I'm sorry…"

"It's okay, sweetie, I know where your heart is." Celeste kissed her daughter on the cheek. She smoothed the hair back from her youngest daughter's face. She was very blessed to have such a wonderful family, an adoring husband, and four beautiful daughters. And, because Dolly was pregnant, they had a grandchild on the way. If only…

"Working today, Mike?'

"Going to the museum with Brooke and her sister, DeeAnn." He actually was looking forward to the day. He really liked museums.

"Huh," was all Will said, but that said a lot.

"It should be fun. He could tell that Will didn't agree. Besides they have the King Tut exhibit there right now."

"Oh, yeah, Randi's supposed to go to that today. I just remembered." Will cast a look toward Mike to see his reaction.

The day was looking better and better.

Will saw Mike's smile and knew his friend had it bad for Randi. He wondered if she felt the same. Interesting. He didn't know how he felt about Mike liking Randi in that way. Mike seemed like a real nice fella, but Randi – she was their little sister. They didn't want her getting hurt.

Mike – with the other three bodyguards, Rick, Charlie, and Brandon – rode in the limousine with the two girls in the center of the seats. The men sat near the windows so they could watch out for any danger. There was still plenty of room on the seats, so they were all comfortable. They talked lightly about the weather and other small talk until they reached the museum. Brooke looked especially cute today in jeans and a soft pink sweater, while DeeAnn had dressed up a little more in a beautifully cut pale lavender pant suit. The girls were really beautiful. He wondered why DeeAnn kept herself at such arms length from Charlie and Jeff. They both had a thing for her, but she wouldn't even look at Jeff when he was around. Charlie fared little better.

Mike slid out with the other bodyguards to survey the area before the presidential daughters were allowed to exit the car. They hurried them through the massive front doors into the relative safety of the building.

"Okay, we're in. Come back for us about noon," Mike told the limousine driver.

The six of them made quite a stir as they made their way through the museum and the Tut exhibit. Mike struck up a conversation with DeeAnn about college and the kind of courses she was taking. She was very open and shared some of her dreams of being a lawyer. She seemed very focused for a nineteen-year old girl. The statuesque DeeAnn and the more slender petite Brooke caused quite a few male heads to turn. It was for sure that DeeAnns' bodyguard, Charlie, had noticed how pretty she was. He could tell that Charlie didn't like Mike getting so close to DeeAnn. Mike smiled to himself. Charlie had nothing to worry about. Mike had eyes for only one girl. A gorgeous blonde with sky blue eyes. He kept searching for her but never saw her any time while in the exhibit. He was surprised at just how disappointed he was not to catch a glimpse of her. Even in the King Tut exhibit their paths never crossed. Mike scolded himself for acting like such a teenager.

Brooke and DeeAnn insisted they wanted to see everything in the whole museum, but noon came and they were only half way through.

"Are we ready?" Mike spoke to the group, but Brooke answered.

"I'm ready. I wanted to see more, but I guess there will be other days." She swept a loose lock of blonde hair behind her ear and started forward. Mike had to grab her arm to keep her from getting ahead of him out the door. Mike paused at the entrance to make sure everyone was ready.

"Drew, we're on our way out." Mike led the group through the large double doors and toward the limousine parked right in front. Just as he opened the door to let Brooke in the backseat, he heard a ping against the top of the car.

"What was…?" Brooke didn't get to finish the question before Mike was yelling for the other guards to get the girls in the reinforced car. He knew immediately what it was. Someone was shooting at them, and they had to be using a silenced rifle. There was no telling where the shooter was. As he was shoving Brooke into the seat, a searing pain rolled across the side of his head. He stumbled a little as he was closing the door and Brooke looked back at him. A gasp escaped her throat and she tried to open her door to check on him.

"No! Stay in the car."

"But…"

"Charlie, get them out of here then call it in!"

Within minutes the place was crawling with police and secret service agents. The president had been called and informed of the incident and assured that his daughters were fine and being transported back to the White House.

The media was not far behind the police vehicles, and a strand of yellow tape was strung around the perimeter to keep them and the onlookers out. Police were assigned different areas to search and the secret service agents began questioning onlookers. No one could tell them anything.

Mike had been taken to the hospital despite his assurances that he was okay.

Riding in the back of the ambulance, he went over everything they had done that morning and everything he could remember about those last few moments.

Josh Key, the Director of the Secret Service, rode in the ambulance with him. He had been close by when the call had come in from the White House. When he pulled up and saw the ambulance, his heart dropped like a stone. He didn't know anyone had been hurt. He found Mike sitting at the back of the ambulance. Apparently a bullet had grazed the side of his head. A fair amount of blood, but head wounds do that. At least he was awake and talking, that was promising. He climbed in the ambulance with Mike and situated himself in the corner out of the way of the EMTs.

The Secret Service Director was tall and broad shouldered with a slender waist. Under his expensive suit, his muscles bulged as a testament to the care he took to keep in shape. He had a little trouble getting himself far enough in the corner to keep out of the way.

Just the fact it was the Director in the ambulance with Mike was an indication of the seriousness of the situation. Mike leaned his head to one side so the EMT tech could wipe some of the blood from his wound to get an idea of how serious it was.

"Gonna need some stitches, looks like," the EMT – Jag, his friend called him – said to the other EMT, Emit. Fortyish and with one of those faces only a mother could love, Emit seemed to know his business. He peered at the long bloody crease across Mike's head and pursed his lips.

"Better get him on to the hospital. Get him checked out."

"Mike, is there anything you can think of? Anyone paying too much attention to the girls? Or anyone you saw in more than one place…think back."

"Mr. Key. I…I've thought about it and I just can't think of anything. It seemed to come out of the blue. He touched the side of his head and winced.

"I'm sorry. I know you're in pain."

"No, I'm okay. I just wish I could give you some place to start. The only thing I can tell you is what direction I think the bullets came from, but your team will be able to tell you that."

Josh agreed with Mike. They would have the best technicians going over every inch of pavement, buildings, webcams, you name it, until they could find out who did this. Everyone in the vicinity would be interviewed. Measurements would be taken and assessed. All the buildings in the area with a possibility of having been used for the shooting would be checked for bullet casings, fingerprints, even gun shot residue.

The ambulance barreled down the street toward the hospital, but Mike was hardly aware of its motion he was so caught up in trying to remember any little detail to help find the shooter.

CHAPTER 30

"I can't believe you. You missed? You're supposed to be the very best. That's what I paid for." Bob Meeker was steaming mad. "Now they will be watching carefully. You could have had it done, but instead you failed. If you think I'm going to pay for this, you're out of your mind!" They had met in an abandoned warehouse in one of the more run-down areas of D.C. Bob hated all this cloak and dagger stuff but he couldn't afford to be seen with this man. The man had a record as a hit man for the mob. He was a dangerous man, but Bob wasn't worried. Money talked, loudly. And he could tell this man wanted to listen.

He looked every bit the part. Heavyset, pitted face, dark swarthy complexion. He looked mean, but he also had an air of being very astute. His dark suit was very plain, but the quality attested to just how well he was paid for the things he did. He had to be smart, at least about his job. Evading jail sentences and lawsuits for many years took someone intelligent or at least very street-smart.

"I will get the job done. It'll take a little longer to let the dust settle, but what else are you going to do? Do it yourself?" The burly man in front of him smiled a hateful smile.

"I don't do those things. That's what I pay men like you for." Bob got in his own jab. "It needs to be done very soon. Time is running out." He left the man standing there and got into the car he had rented for the meeting. It was your basic dark blue rent-a-car, non-descript, not easily traced, especially since he had taken the time to daub mud on the license plate. He knew better than to use his own car. Bob was taking no chances of being connected to this man in any way. Now he had to go and face Hadley, something he abso-lutely dreaded.

"Horace, he promised to get it done. We don't have a lot of choice here," Bob assured him. Meeker cringed at the glare Hadley sent his way. The man was losing it.

"He had better get it done soon. That young man is too close to the president. What if he realizes who he is? All he would have to do is hand those photos over to his *Daddy* and that would be the end of me, and my bid for the presidency. He glanced up in time to see Meeker's smirk before it was wiped off his face. "And the end of you, Bob. You know I won't go down by myself," and smiled as his campaign manager paled. Hadley paced back and forth across the room with long strides. He pounded his fist into his other hand as a release to his fury. He'd like to pound it into Meeker's head. What a mess.

"Just a thought. This Calloway was grazed on the head. It wasn't a kill shot, but what if he took a turn for the worse while at home? That might not be too suspicious."

"You're thinking maybe an accident…poison? Maybe a bad prescription." Hadley's hopes were up a little. Maybe things were going to work out for him after all. He eased back in his office chair and thought of all he would do when he was president of the United States. That had such a nice ring to it…Horace Hadley, President of *the* United States. When he came out of his musing he realized that Meeker was still in his office looking at him questioningly.

"Get out of here and get something done!" His bark caused Meeker to jerk to his feet like strings had pulled him straight up. When Meeker thought about it, he realized that was just what it was, strings. And Hadley was pulling them.

CHAPTER 31

At the hospital, the doctors who examined Mike after the shooting incident were trying to decide what had taken place. At first glance it seemed clear cut. One fairly deep gouge where the bullet had luckily just grazed his head. On the other hand they had the CAT scan. It looked like the bullet was lodged in the back part of his brain. It didn't make sense. They x-rayed several angles trying to get some answers, but it was still a mystery. They finally decided they needed some help figuring out the puzzle so they called in a couple of forensics docs that had years of experience in such cases for the police.

While Mike patiently waited for them to treat the cut, two other doctors came to examine his head. That was a little weird. It was just a scratch compared to some injuries he had had over his years in the marines, and he had never had four doctors attending to him. Still, he couldn't do anything but look around at the four sterile white walls until they finished with him. Of course there were a couple of really pretty nurses that came by to check on him every few minutes. One took the opportunity to check his pulse every time, giving him a smile and batting her long eyelashes at him. She was a really cute redhead with a killer smile. For some reason Will popped into his thoughts. Hmmm…

"Did you hear what happened? It's all over the news. Someone tried to shoot the president's daughters." Jeff was pouring himself some cornflakes when Will burst in the kitchen. Half the cornflakes landed on the table.

"What! When?"

"Today. While we were up in the mountains camping."

All the color drained from Jeff's face, "Which ones? Are they alright?"

Will had forgotten that Jeff had a major crush on DeeAnn. "Hold on, sorry. They're okay. It was DeeAnn and Brooke." At Jeff's sick look, Will grabbed his shoulder. "Hey, they're okay. Now our roommate, he didn't fair so well. He's okay, just a graze to the head but they kept him overnight at the hospital for observation."

Jeff felt his heart begin to beat right again. He was ashamed at how glad he was that it wasn't DeeAnn that was hit. Then he thought of Mike and how they had become pretty good friends over the last few weeks.

"Hey, bro. Let's cut to the hospital and pay our respects."

"They've probably released him already, don't ya think?"

"Call and find out."

"I think they took him to George Washington." Will picked up the phone to call and looked over at Jeff.

"They haven't released him yet. I wonder what's goin' on." Will put the phone back in its cradle and picked up his keys. "Come on. Let's go see what's up." Jeff slapped his brother on the back and followed him out of the apartment.

"Should we call Randi?" Jeff knew that Will was even more protective of Randi than he was.

"She'd probably be mad if we didn't. You saw how she was with him the other day." Jeff nodded his head. Yeah, he had seen. He didn't think Randi had realized just how much showed in her eyes, but her brothers knew her too well. She was smitten.

"Cole, I don't know what's going on." Mel calmly walked over to where the President stood at the window. "The FBI has been on this from right after it happened. They can't figure it out either. Why would anyone target your girls? Kidnap? Sure…but kill? That's just crazy. Can you think of any reason? Maybe an old boyfriend? You haven't gotten any threats against them. We've checked."

"So… *why*? Why out of the blue would someone take potshots at my girls?" Cole was so mad and frustrated he could barely think. Maybe that's what they were trying to do. "Do you think this could be about the campaign? Would someone do that just to throw me off? Get me to reconsider running?"

"Anyone with any sense would know it was too late for that." Mel worried about his friend. His family meant more to him than anything else...even the presidency. He loved this man like a brother and had always been made to feel a part of this family. He was as protective of his friend's daughters as he would be his own daughter...if she had lived past infancy. He had never told Cole about the little girl. She had died in a fire when she was only a couple of months old. A suspicious fire. Her mother's body was not found anywhere in the house. He never heard from her again. It seemed as if she vanished off the face of the earth. After that he never could bring himself to get close to anyone in that way again. He filled his life with helping Cole and his family. He tried to be the best Vice-President he could be and work for the country he loved.

Cole agreed that it was too late to back out of the race, but that still left the question of *why*? Why the girls and not him?

"Mel, I want to go see the young man that took care of my girls. I want to thank him...personally."

"Of course, Cole. I'll call Josh and get him on it." He knew that was coming. Cole was a good man and would want to do right by the young man...*Mike? Yes, that's the name. Mike Calloway.*

Mike was tired of this hospital room. Why would they not let him go? Oh, everyone was nice, but he couldn't stand this lying around any longer. He picked up the remote and flipped through the channels. He finally settled on a news channel. There were a few snips of information on the attack on the girls, but they still had no one in custody and very little to go on.

The door opened and one of his doctors, Dr. Yawn, filled the narrow space. He beamed a kind smile as he sat in a chair by the bed. Mike could imagine patients putting their full trust in this man with the flowing white hair.

"Well, young man, I've been given the job of telling you what's going on."

"Great! It's about time someone did." Mike straightened up a little in the bed, ready to finally get his release.

"Ah, yes, I'm sure it been confusing. You'll have to understand how confusing it's been for us as your doctors." At Mike's frown, Dr. Yawn launched into the explanation as far as they had been able to figure out.

"Young man, Mike…may I call you Mike?" The doctor spent a few moments cleaning the lenses of his glasses with a soft cloth he had taken from his pocket.

"Sure."

"Yes, well, Mike, you've caused quite a stir. I can say in my thirty years as a physician I have not come across anyone who has been shot in the head twice and lived to tell about it." He said it with almost gleeful laughter in his voice.

"No, that's not right. I was only hit once. The other shot was several feet away and hit the top of the car." Mike pulled the covers back and swung his legs around so he could sit facing the doctor. He noticed the doctor's slightly bushy eyebrows rise.

"Yes, yesterday. But are you aware that you have a bullet lodged in your brain?" He reached and touched the back of Mike's head. "Mm...right about here?"

Mike looked at him dumbfounded. "What...what... I...no way. Wouldn't I know something like that? Wouldn't I have some kind of problems...symptoms?"

"Funny thing about the brain. At times it can be very mysterious. All we can figure is that at some point in your young life you were shot in the head with a small caliber gun. At the time you may have been disoriented for a while, maybe some headaches, then the site healed over and the brain encapsulated the bullet. If you did not for some reason seek medical attention, you may not have known why you were hurting. Is there a time that you may have been shot at? Probably a few years ago going by how the long the bullet appears to have been in your head. Maybe a gang fight or some such?"

"No, I was never a part of a gang...at least I don't think so." Mike hesitated.

"Surely, you would know if you were part of a gang?" Dr. Yawn seemed so easy to talk to that Mike found himself pouring out his story. All the things that had happened. His loss of memory, the couple that had taken him in. Everything came tumbling out like it had been bottled up for too long, which he supposed it had. It took a while for it to sink in what he had just done.

"Please, you can't tell anyone. You're my doctor, right? This is confidential information, isn't it?" Mike was afraid that if anyone knew of his amnesia it would bring unwanted attention to him. His old fears returned to haunt him.

Dr. Yawn had to warn him that he was not the only one who knew about the other bullet. The FBI also had that information and they would probably be asking him about it. He advised him to tell them exactly the same thing he had just told him. They could find out who he really was.

"No, I don't need to know...I can't know." Now he really was agitated and Dr. Yawn called a nurse to give him a small sedative. Something was going on with this young man. He just hoped it was not something bad that he had done. He seemed like such a nice young man. If he had done something bad, he had to have been pretty young. What was he now...only twenty-six?

"Now, now, don't you worry. It'll be all right." He patted the young man's hand. "Did you know the president was asking about you?"

"The president?"

"Yes, he was asking how you were doing. Said you took one for his daughters. He was very proud of you and thankful that you were going to be okay." Dr. Yawn had divulged that information hoping to take the young man's mind off whatever it was making him so upset. It worked, thank goodness, because he also had some other information that was going to be upsetting as well.

"Mike, I know you're not going to want to hear this, but it has to be said." He hesitated and looked at the young man before him.

"Okay...more bad news?"

Dr. Yawn took a deep breath and let it out in a sigh, "That bullet needs to come out."

"You mean brain surgery? Is that really necessary? I mean it's been there for a while, you said. Can't it just stay there as long as it's not causing any problems?"

"I wish you didn't have to go through this, son, but it looks like the second bullet's impact, even though it was just a scrape, may have caused the first bullet to move. It's got to come out or it could cause even more damage."

"When…when would I need this done?"

Dr. Yawn reached over and squeezed Mike's arm reassuringly. "I can set it up for tomorrow, give you a little time to pray about it. Also, the president wants to speak with you. It's being quietly arranged for after normal visiting hours are over."

When the door popped open a little while later, Mike was surprised to see Jeff and Will peering in at him. "Oh good. You're awake." Will came all the way into the room waving his hand back toward the door at Jeff to come in, too.

"Hi. What are you two up to?" Mike laughed as they produced a bag of burgers and some cokes.

"Thought you could use some comfort food. I know what most hospital food is like." He bowed as he presented the bag to Mike.

"Thanks, you two."

It was a great thought, but he couldn't tell them he might not be able to eat any of it, or anything else. Not if he was having surgery tomorrow.

Jeff moved over to the chair by the bed. "Are you okay, Mike?"

After the briefest of hesitations, Mike looked over at the brothers. Should he tell them? They shared an apartment. Whatever happened to him could affect them, too. Before he could tell them, the door opened again and there was Randi. Wow, and did she ever look great. Her hair fell softly around her face and down onto her shoulders. Her eyes rivaled the sky blue of her top, and she had on jeans that made her legs look long and slender and *wow*!

"If I had known you guys were coming here I would've ridden with you." Randi hugged each one and then stood by the side of the bed. She looked a bit nervous being there.

"Randi…" After that, words failed him. His mouth dried up and all coherent thought left.

"How are you?" Her voice was soft and musical. He could listen to it for hours. Did he have it bad or what?

"I'm, um, fine. A little headache, but that's all."

"Brooke was beside herself with worry. She begged her parents to let her come with me but the Secret Service guys said no way. All the girls are being kept close right now. DeeAnn wasn't even allowed to go to class." Randi touched the back of his hand with her long fingers. "I'm so glad you're alright. Brooke asked me to tell you to get better soon. She misses her favorite bodyguard."

He laughed at that. Maybe he had finally gotten the President's youngest daughter to trust him. That would certainly make his job easier. That is if he still had a job after all this was over. He tried to swallow the lump that had formed in his throat.

A nurse stuck her head in the door and smiled at the three visitors. "I'm sorry, but visiting hours are over."

"Thanks for coming by, guys, and thanks for the food." Will and Jeff had munched on the burgers while he and Randi were talking.

"But you didn't eat any of it. We ate it all. Besides, you were going to tell us something…and I think it must have been important." Will didn't like the vibes he was getting. Something was up. Jeff gave him that look that always said, *Shut up, Will.*

As they filed out of the room, Mike wanted to call them back and tell them. Have them pray for him. He felt so alone.

I will never leave you or forsake you.

Mike heard the words in his head. "Thank you, God, for being with me right now. I needed you to comfort me and strengthen me."

His head was still bowed when the door opened and two men came in and quickly scanned the room. Secret Service. Both were in their thirties, well built and armed with pistols under their jackets.

One of the men spoke quietly into a microphone at his wrist, and the door opened again.

"How are you doing, Mike?" This time it was President Harris who took the chair by his bed.

"I'm fine, sir."

"Aw, come on, son, tell me the truth. You've been shot in the head, spent most of two days in the hospital eating hospital food, had very little company. I want to know how you really are…no punches pulled, okay?"

Mike bit back a smile. The man sounded like he really cared. It made Mike want to open up and spill everything.

"I guess I've had better days than this."

"You know I can never thank you enough for getting my girls out of harm's way so quickly. I…" Words failed him. He loved his daughters so much that the thought of losing one or both was just impossible to accept. Especially after the loss of his only son.

"I just wish I could've prevented it…seen it coming in time." Mike fidgeted with his covers. He scanned the president's face for the condemnation he felt would be there, but his face showed only compassion.

President Harris looked at the young man for several moments. His eyes scanned the young man's nice-looking face, took in his trim but well muscled body. He was surprised his girls hadn't swooned over him. Maybe the last couple of bodyguards had made them a little more wary.

"Believe me, son, there wasn't anything you could've done. The FBI and the Secret Service guys have all been looking at this thing from every angle possible and it just doesn't make sense. Even the angle of the bullets was all strange."

"Strange? Strange how?" Mike raised up in the bed so he could see the president's face better.

Cole wasn't sure the FBI was okay with him spilling too much information, but he wanted to tell this young man something that would make him be more on his guard.

"Mike, they think the trajectory was all wrong for the shooter to have been aiming at the girls."

"I'm sorry. I don't understand, sir. Why do they think that? What else would they have been aiming at?"

"Not what," he hesitated, "Whom." Realizing he had lost him, Cole sighed.

"Mike, they think you may have been the primary target."

Mike could only gape at the man in front of him. The idea that he was the target was ridiculous, but he didn't want to outright laugh in the face of the President.

"Sir, I…with all due respect…I don't see that as possible. Why would anyone target me? What reason could anyone have to hurt me?"

"I hate to have to tell you this, but those are questions the FBI and Secret Service is going to be asking you soon. They will probably grill you for quite a while about your life, family, old girlfriends, etc. Please be honest and straightforward with them."

"Yes, sir, but they may have to wait a while." He could see the question forming in the President's eyes, so he told him about the bullet he was scheduled to have removed the next day.

"Of all the strange things I've heard, that beats them all. You must have nine lives like a cat, young man. Or have someone watching over you."

"I don't think it's luck, sir." Cole nodded and stood up to leave.

"Mike, I'll be praying for the surgery and for a quick recovery. If there is anything you need, just call. I'll make sure they know to put your call through to me."

"Thank you, sir." He couldn't believe it, a straight line to the president of the United States. If only his parents could have lived to see this day. They would have been thrilled. He still missed them so much. They had been wonderful parents, firm but understanding, generous but not spoiling, and always supportive. He had come to love them so much in the short time they had together.

Why did everything with her brothers have to be so hard to plan? Randi wanted to meet with them at the hospital this morning. She had found out about Mike's surgery from Will last night. He had called right after Mike had called to let the boys know and asked them to pray for him. Her brothers were running late and she didn't want them to take Mike to surgery without her seeing him first. Just so she could pray with him she told herself. Not because she was scared to death she would never be able to speak to him again or anything like that. Yeah, right.

She quietly knocked on the door, "Are you decent?"

Mike's head jerked toward the door. He didn't know Randi would be coming by this early in the morning. He hadn't even combed his hair, but it was too late for that now. "Yeah, come on in." She had on a white skirt that reached almost to her knees, and a multi-colored top with short sleeves. The colors were all pastels and enhanced the color of her blue eyes.

He would never get tired of the sight of her. She looked…worried? *Oh no. Her brothers told her about the operation.* That's why she was here so early.

"They told you, didn't they?" He could see it in her perfect heart-shaped face.

"I'm sorry. If you thought my brothers could keep a secret you were sadly misinformed. Everyone who knows them knows to wait until time to leave for a surprise party before telling them. They can't really help it – they are just so open with people. The only closely guarded secrets are the ones the kids tell them in their youth group meetings. Those are held as sacred." She smiled at him and his heart did a flip.

"It's okay. I'm…I'm glad you're here. There's something I wanted to ask you." He had taken her hand in his. He loved the feel of her hand. It was so soft, so fragile. He looked up at her beautiful face. "I would like…"

"Hey! Sorry we're late, got held up in this awful traffic jam." Will barreled into the room with his usual zest.

Great timing, Will, Mike thought to himself.

Jeff came in at a more modest pace but stopped as soon as he saw Randi's hand in Mike's. "What's going on?" Mike saw the frown on Jeff's face and realized it was because he still had a hold on Randi's hand. Randi's quick thinking covered for him, telling her brothers that she and Mike were about to pray without them since they were so late.

The brothers looked duly scolded and Jeff seemed to accept Randi's explanation.

CHAPTER 32

"Horace, we might have our problems solved."

Bob Meeker had called as soon as he found out about the surgery. "I've got it in place. By tonight or tomorrow at the latest we'll be home free. No one will be able to tell that it wasn't caused by this surgery the boy is having to remove the bullet you put there."

"Don't tell me about it! Idiot. This line is not secure! I don't need to know anything about it except that it's done." *The fool. Why did I ever think I could use this man? He's going to blow the whole thing with his big mouth.*

"Okay, okay. I'll get back with you." Bob slammed the phone down and left the room fuming mad, muttering to himself. "Calling me an idiot. Yeah, he's right – an idiot for ever getting involved in his campaign. Well, this is the end of that. After this I'm out." He stormed down the hallway and out of the building, his footsteps pounding loudly, causing several people to turn and stare after him. Mel Myers had rounded the corner of the hallway just as Meeker was stomping his was toward the door.

Mel gazed at Meeker's retreating back, thinking that that was a time bomb about to go off. Maybe this situation needed a little checking out.

CHAPTER 33

Dr. Yawn had already been by Mike's room early in the morning and explained a little more of what was going to be done during the surgery. He gave him a little background on the Dr. Smithson that would be performing the surgery. Apparently, the President had made a special request for the best surgeon to be heading the operation. Before he left, Dr. Yawn even prayed with Mike.

As they rolled Mike down the hallway toward the operating room, he thought of all the prayers said over him and was overwhelmed at the feeling of peace that flooded his heart and mind. He knew that whatever happened in the operating room, God was with him. Everything would work out.

"This is one weird case." Dr. Smithson looked down at the young man whose head he was operating on. They were trying out some new techniques to lessen the recovery time from surgical procedures. Less invasive surgery where only the area affected was opened up with as small an opening as possible. It was tedious and you had to have a very steady hand, but it was worth it to the patient. Less recovery time and less disfigurement were their goals. That there was less chance of infection was a bonus. The surgery seemed to go perfectly and he was glad that he could tell the President that his young soldier should make a full recovery. He thanked God every day for the skills that he was given. Reminding himself where his skill came from kept him humble. He knew that many doctors get 'God complexes' because they believe they are responsible for healing. They forget, until they lose a patient whose surgery goes bad despite every thing the surgeon tries to prevent it, that God is in control, not them.

"Mike…Mike? Can you hear me?" The anesthesiologist kept jiggling Mike's hand, trying to get him to come around after the surgery. The quicker he came out the better his prognosis would be.

A small moan and a quick opening of his eyes was all Mike could give him before he was back under, but it was enough to satisfy the doctor for now. As soon as he came around enough, they would extract the tube from his throat and get him into a room.

The surgeon, Dr. Smithson, came by to check on him one more time before he went to inform the group of people in the waiting room. As he understood it, the young man had no family. But he seemed to have a lot of friends pulling for him. He even had the president of the United States waiting for an update on his condition. He had better call him first and then deal with the folks in the waiting room.

"What's taking so long? He's been out of surgery for two hours." Will was pacing the small waiting room floor, jostling the change in the pocket of his white chinos, and making everyone else tense.

Charlie and Rick sat a little apart from the others, quietly discussing the ongoing investigation and the lack of evidence they'd come up with as they waited for word on Mike's surgery.

"I'm sure he's okay or we would've heard. Don't you think?" Even Randi could hear the worry in her own voice. She needed to know how Mike was…that he was going to be okay. She had seen him in a very different light this morning before the surgery. He had been calm, even teasing her and her brothers. Praying with him and for him had been a joy. It was such a shame he had no family. She loved her family so much and couldn't imagine her life without them.

A door opened at the side of the waiting room, and the doctor that did Mike's surgery walked over to them. It was a good sign that he was smiling as he approached. He was a good-looking man and Randi felt his eyes linger on her a little longer than necessary.

"Are you the friends of Mike Calloway?"

Everyone answered yes at the same time and the doctor chuckled a little.

"I'm glad the young man has so many good friends. Now, Mr. Calloway gave us permission to tell his

friends everything about his surgery and prognosis."
Dr. Smithson looked at each one of the young people
surrounding him. "I've also talked with the president, at
his request." Realizing that everyone was waiting he got
on with the explanation. "The surgery went very well.
He is a healthy young man, in great shape, and that
helps his prognosis tremendously. Still, we are talking
brain surgery. We really can't know the extent of damage from removal of the bullet or the extent of damage the bullet had caused while it was there. From the
indications we've seen this morning, we think it will
be minimal. You may see a few odd moments, maybe a
little forgetfulness. These should go away with time. As
his friends, I would ask that you try to get him to take
it easy for a while. Are there any questions?"

"How long will he have to stay in the hospital?"

The doctor looked over at the gorgeous young
woman who asked the question. She obviously cared a
great deal for the patient.

"A week or two depending on how he progresses."

"Will he need care after he gets out?"

"If he does well, other than taking things easy, he
should be able to get by on his own. Except for driving.
No driving for at least three weeks. Until we can be sure
there will be no seizures or blackouts." He raised his
eyebrows to ask for any further questions. Jeff reached
out to shake his hand.

"Thank you for taking good care of Mike for us."

"You're welcome, and if he has any problems, have
him call me immediately. He's one lucky man to have
so many friends to care about him."

CHAPTER 34

He thought the nurse would never leave. She kept messing with the antibiotic drip, the pillow, straightening things on the side table. She must have her eye on the young man. Eh, she was a looker, with that red hair. He was always partial to redheads. But he needed to get in that room unseen and get the job done.

Finally, the girl left the young man's bedside. As soon as she rounded the corner, Casio came out of the small room across the hall where he was hiding. Thankfully she had left the door open the whole time so he could watch her. The burly man in hospital mask and gown looked around one more time before entering the room. No one even looked his way. This was going to be a snap.

As he eased over to the side of the bed, he thought the young man might have opened his eyes. When he reached into his pocket and drew out the syringe he had prepared beforehand, the door opened and a young woman and man entered the room without knocking.

"Oh, sorry, we were told we could come in for just a couple of minutes."

"That's okay. I'll just come back later." The man said in a very quiet voice like he was trying not to disturb the patient. What he was really doing was trying to keep anyone from being able to identify his voice if this all went sour. It was all he could do to walk slowly out of the room.

"Thank you. Are you one of Mike's doctors? I don't think I've met you." Randi was eyeing the man suspiciously. Something seemed off about the man, but she couldn't put her finger on it.

Casio just wanted to get out of that room but he had to give her an answer.

"No, not a regular doctor. I was asked to do a consult." With that he made his escape.

"Wow, look at all these tubes and wires. It looks like aliens have taken over his body for experiments." Will made his way around the bed, looking at all the hookups and gadgets.

Randi laughed. Will had a funny way of looking at things sometimes, but he was right – it did look a little alien to have all these things hooked up to your body. Poor Mike. She hated all this for him. She reached over and took hold of his hand and felt comforted by that small touch. Will noticed her action but didn't comment.

"Umm, hi…" Mike tried to turn his head toward the person who had taken his hand but his head felt like it was in a vise.

"Hi, Mike. How are you feeling?"

Randi! "I…uh. I think I'm okay." His voice was scratchy from the tube that had been inserted down his throat. He finally got his head to turn enough so he could see her, even though moving sent pains shooting down the base of his skull to his neck and shoulders. *Man, does she look nice.*

"Do you need anything? Maybe a drink of water? Only a sip or two, okay?"

"Yes, thanks." He took one sip, then another, and then Randi took the straw away from his mouth.

"Thanks for coming to see me."

Will stepped closer to the bed so Mike could see him easier without having to turn his head.

"Will, Randi… I appreciate your family being here for me. It means a lot."

"Hey, we're friends. And I'm your brother in Christ. Ahem, that makes Randi your sister, too." As he said that last part he laughed out loud at Mike and Randi's expressions.

Out of the hospital in less than a week after brain surgery? Amazing. Casio had tried three other times to get in and every time one of those pesky kids was in there. How was he supposed to get the job done when the guy's friends kept hovering over him? Of course, Meeker was beside himself. Casio had not lived up to his reputation. He would…because he wanted that money. Now, it was an even bigger payoff. He had *talked* Meeker into increasing the amount. Of course, Meeker had little choice in the matter. Casio hoped this payoff would put him in a position to get out of the United States. Start a new life in some country where his money would go much further. Maybe Mexico or Costa Rica.

Now he would have to look for another opportunity to get this guy. That meant he would have to trail around after him. He hated that. Such a waste of time. Plus, he was much more likely to get caught and that was unacceptable. Casio was through being someone else's tool. He wanted a life, a real life where he didn't have to always look over his shoulder. Where he wasn't always just one step ahead of the police.

CHAPTER 35

Horace Hadley was in a snit. The poles showed a drop in his ratings against Harris. What could he do to fix it? The man seemed immune to any criticism.

Maybe he could get some photos of him and get one of his computer gurus to fix them up. It wouldn't work for long, but maybe long enough to get through the election next month. Meeker better be taking care of their other problem soon. He would get Meeker on the photo thing right away, too.

"No! No. I've done all I'm going to do of your dirty work. I'm sick of it." Meeker just shrugged when Hadley reminded him of the document. He didn't care anymore. He was in a spot either way he went. One way or the other, he was going to get caught. If he got out now, maybe he could at least salvage something of a life. It would just be without his wife, or her money, or his family. What a depressing thought. How had it come to this? One thing. He had done one bad thing and tried to cover it up. But that one thing led to another and, after Hadley found out, another and so on. Somehow he had allowed a snake like Hadley to get a firm hold his throat.

Hadley knew Meeker was getting cold feet, but he was in too far now to get out. He would make sure Meeker did what he was supposed to. Besides the document in his pocket, he had other ways of making sure old Bob toed the line. Some of them very painful. He hadn't gotten to where he was by letting things just happen. He made things happen…his way. If he had to, he would take care of Meeker. It wouldn't be the first time he had gotten rid of someone standing in his way. That was the cause of his problems right now – that boy with the camera so many years ago. Almost ten years. He had had to do a lot of damage control that night. The two officers with him had gotten cold feet, but he warned them what would happen if one of them said a word to anyone. They knew better than to cross Hadley. They had helped hold the man while Hadley shot him in the head. They had to back Hadley's story or they would implicate themselves. He didn't have anything to worry about there. One of them was so old he was probably already dead, and if the other kept drinking like he was when Hadley last *visited* him, then he should be dead, too.

CHAPTER 36

"Mike!" Brooke sailed across the room and flung herself into Mike's arms. "I'm so glad you're back." Brooke couldn't believe what she had just done. She turned a deep red all the way to her hairline. "Sorry. I just really missed you. The other guys are okay but…" She was digging the hole deeper and deeper.

"Thanks, Brooke. It's nice to know I was missed." He turned to say hello to Brooke's mother and gave Brooke time to get over her embarrassment. Even though he thought it was pretty cute how she had flung herself at him.

"How are you doing, Mike?" Celeste laid her hand on his arm in a friendly gesture.

"I'm doing really well. Better than they expected me to do in such a short time."

She hoped he was able to come back to work soon. Brooke had been so much better with him than she was with any of the other bodyguards. She couldn't believe the change in her daughter since the shooting. She seemed a little more grown up. Some of that was good, but she didn't want her daughter to grow up too soon.

She wanted her to remain in that childhood innocence for a few more years.

"No lasting affects?"

He gave a small shake of his head. He didn't want to lie to the president's wife, but he wasn't going to get into his problems with her either. After the surgery, Mike had been having more and more dreams... dreams of being chased, afraid. It was beginning to affect his sleep. There were shadows under his eyes that had not been there when he got out of the hospital.

"None that I can't handle." His response was the truth. With God's help, he could handle whatever came his way.

"Mike, can you have dinner with us? Mom said it would be okay. Please."

Celeste couldn't believe the change in her daughter's attitude. Never would she have asked such a thing before. Now she was pleading for this young man's company?

"Ah, sure, that would be nice, thank you. That is, if you're sure Mrs. Harris."

Maybe he had sensed her hesitation, but she really did want to get to know him better. After all, he did save her daughters' lives. She smiled and reassured him that it was what they wanted.

They relaxed in the West Wing Sitting Room where many Presidential families before them had spent their family time while they waited for their meal to be prepared by the White House chef.

It was beautifully decorated with many original pieces and some pieces that former presidents' wives had added. He could tell that Mrs. Harris had probably changed only a few things – added a few of their personal items, such as pictures of the girls and themselves. The billowing yellow curtains were probably her addition as well. They gave the room a lighter airy feel contrasting with the heavier, dark, antique furniture.

"Tell me about yourself, Mike. Where did you grow up?" Celeste settled into a comfortable sofa beside her daughter. Brooke scooted closer to her and linked her arm in her mother's. Before he could answer, the other three Harris girls came in and settled around their mother and sister.

After they were settled, Celeste looked at Mike, still expecting an answer to her questions. He knew she wasn't trying to pry into his life. She was just interested. Because of that he gave her a brief background of his life with the Calloways. He told them how he was home schooled and earned his degree from Cal Tech at twenty years old. When he told them about the freak accident that took his parents from him, he could feel their sympathy.

"I wasn't sure what to do after that. I missed them so much. The Marine recruiting office was close to the Cal Tech campus and I guess I just passed it at the right time."

After a delicious dinner served in the family dining room, everyone went back into to the sitting area for coffee and dessert. Mike enjoyed watching the sisters' banter back and forth about movies, clothes, and of course young men. Brooke dominated the conversation with DeeAnn coming in a distant second. He really enjoyed listening to Dolly. She had been around more and knew more of the workings of the capital, even though she was not very involved in politics. Madeline was the quietest. He wasn't sure if that was just the way she was or if she didn't particularly care for him. He caught her glancing his way several times during the evening with a slight frown on her face.

"DeeAnn and Brooke told him things about Randi that made him smile. He didn't realize the families had know each other for several years before the Harris family moved to the White House. Randi's Dad had been Ambassador to the U.N. for several years. Her Mom was an interpreter for the White House, so Randi had been in contact with many of the children of White House staff and other support staff. Some of the Congressmen and Senator's children had attended the same schools as she and her brothers. DeeAnn and Randi had become friends on their first day of school. She became like the sister Randi had always wanted.

All evening, Mike and the girls kept a conversation going back and forth, some of it teasing and sometimes talking about current topics and school. Mike had a good grasp of many areas because he had traveled so much. Dolly couldn't believe he had such an under-standing of art. She invited him to come over some day to her husband Louis's studio. She explained that it was her husband's studio even though both their names were on the door. Louis took care of the everyday run-ning of the studio and Dolly filled the studio with her art. She also engineered all the parties and art shows, inviting various artists to come and show their work.

"When's your next show?" Mike thought it would be nice to see some of Dolly's work.

"In two weeks."

"Would it be alright if I came to it?"

"Please do. I'd like that." Dolly gave him a soft smile.

"Do you realize that boy is having dinner with them right now? What if he tells them something about that night? You were supposed to have this taken care of." Horace Hadley was tired of Meeker's excuses and whining. Horace had some other resources that no one knew about. People who owed him. Now was the time to cash in. If he didn't, it was going to be too late. He already had some other things going that Meeker didn't know about. Pictures. Really good fake pictures of the beautiful Celeste in the arms of another man. He had even found someone he could pay to verify the picture's authenticity, that this person had seen them in the act. How devastating for the president to find out less than a month before the election that his wife is cheating on him and with his best friend and running mate, Mel Meyers. Of course, he'll know they are fakes, and his wife will, but it will take the wind out of his campaign right at a crucial time.

"Get out of here and do something. I want you to call me tomorrow and tell me you've gotten the job done. Do you understand?"

Meeker didn't even answer, just walked out of the office and went to find Casio.

CHAPTER 37

Jeff sat in the kitchen of their apartment brooding. He had a ham sandwich in front of him, but he hadn't even taken a bite yet. All he could think about was the other day when the shooting happened. *What if DeeAnn had been hurt? Killed? He could have lost her.* She wouldn't let him get close to her. Wouldn't even look at him when he spoke to her. He really liked her. *Why wouldn't she even talk to him?* Jeff didn't think he was such an ogre to scare young innocent girls.

Jeff thought of the first time he ever saw DeeAnn. She had been at a party for Randi's thirteenth birthday. At the party there were a bunch of little teen girls giggling and running around the house and DeeAnn was one of them. He had been at college for a year so he hadn't seen her before, even though he had heard about her from Randi. In his superior age of nineteen, he acted like he thought they were all silly little girls. If he had been honest with himself, he had really enjoyed watching the girls in their innocent play. He had felt protective of them the same way he had always been with Randi. He supposed that was when he knew what he wanted to do with his life. He wanted to help kids. Give them someone who was willing to listen and be there for them.

It was that night that he told his parents of his decision to become a youth minister. They were really happy for him and proud of his decision. Will had scowled and stomped off like he was mad. It took a while for him to come clean about why he was so mad. It was because he was hurt that Jeff didn't confide in him first, since they weren't just brothers – they were best buds, too. Jeff was touched that Will felt that way and their relationship remained close ever since.

He'd tried for the last year to get DeeAnn to talk to him. He asked her if she would go out to lunch with him sometime, but she shook her head *no* and ran away. He had even asked Randi if DeeAnn had ever said anything about why she wouldn't go out with him, but Randi said she really didn't know. Any time she mentioned his name, DeeAnn would clam up, only saying she didn't think they were very compatible.

Time to pray about it. Of course, it wouldn't be the first time. He prayed all the time about the girl God had prepared for him. He wanted to make sure he didn't do anything that wasn't in God's plan. That might really mess up his life. He went in to his bedroom and shut the door. He needed to spend some quality time with God.

CHAPTER 38

Cole was furious. He had the morning papers in front of him, shaking them at his public relations officer. "Do something about this. I will not have my wife abused in this way. Or Mel, for that matter. These are so obviously fakes." Never had he been so angry with the media for these blatant lies, this attempt to harm his innocent wife and friend. He never even blinked an eye when the papers were brought to his attention.

The pictures in the Washington Herald and a couple of other papers showed the First Lady in compromising poses with the Vice President. *Fakes*. He knew that, but it still made him want to throw up.

"We've called them. They said they had it on good authority that they were genuine." The public relations man kept backing away as Cole came closer to him.

"Mr. President, we feel it's better if we just tell the people that they are fakes and leave it at that. Those who are going to believe it will believe it and those who won't wouldn't anyway. The people love the First Lady. She's the most popular one America has ever had."

Cole sighed, "You're right, I guess." He thought about it for a few minutes. Going over everything in his mind. "Maybe it would help if Celeste and I were seen out more often together."

There were several dinners and interviews coming up. This close to the election things tended to get very hectic. He would use each opportunity to make sure everyone in the United States knew just how much he loved and trusted his wife. He would make sure everyone could see how he valued and trusted his friend and Vice President. Mel was as close as any brother could be and everyone who knew them at all knew this. The rest didn't matter. The election? If something as contrived as this could sway peoples' opinions that much, then fine. He could find employment elsewhere. Employment with a whole lot less stress attached to it.

"One thing is certain." Cole pinned his public relations officer with a glare.

"Sir?" The man went extremely pale, and Cole thought for a moment that he might pass out.

"If you don't get me the name of the person who 'verified the authenticity' of those pictures, you will no longer have a job here. Do I make that explicit enough?"

"Y…yes, yes, sir," the man stuttered as he turned and practically ran from the room.

CHAPTER 39

Mike was on his way to a little Asian market down a small side street in Chinatown. He had been out of the hospital for over a week and felt really good. He had told Jeff and Will that he wanted to make dinner that evening for them and Randi. They had visited him in the hospital every day that he was there, and they picked him up and brought him back to the apartment, since he wasn't allowed to drive for a couple of weeks. Of course, they said it wasn't necessary to cook them a meal as a thank you, but if he just insisted they would go along with it. They had learned early on that Mike had some awesome cooking skills.

As Mike got close to the building where the market was located, he felt a strange feeling. Was someone following him? He didn't hear any footsteps behind him, but he just had that weird sense that someone was there. Maybe because of all his martial arts training he was more tuned in to such things. As he turned the last corner into the alley he sidestepped close to the building. Two seconds later a large man stepped around the corner of the building, a large knife held down at his right side. He looked surprised to find Mike standing right in front of him.

"Good, good. You make it very easy for me." He raised the knife toward Mike's chest slowly, menacingly.

"Why are you after me?" Mike was preparing his body for action, breathing in and out slowly, relaxing his muscles for that first strike. He would have to be ready. It was obvious this was a man used to fighting. Killing.

The man looked to make sure no one was around, no one looking out their windows with their cell phones trained on him. He slowly made his way toward Mike, holding the knife out in front of him now, waving it just a little trying to get the boy to focus on it. *Ah…the boy was well trained. He keeps watching the eyes.*

"You've caused me a lot of trouble, young man." The man was only a few feet away when he sprang forward with a lightning speed that Mike would have never dreamed possible for such a big man.

Mike's response was just that small amount slower since the brain surgery that the man's knife nicked his shoulder as he dodged out of the way. Now the man was taunting him with the knife like he was confident that he had already won the fight and just wanted to have a little fun before ending it.

"What trouble have I caused you? I don't even know you." If he could get the man to talk, maybe he could distract him enough to get that one opening he needed.

"You shouldn't have survived the first attack. That cost me a lot of pride. I take my work very seriously."

"Work? So someone is paying you to kill me?" Why in the world would someone want to pay to have him killed? "You shot me."

"Now, now. I never talk business when I'm having so much pleasure. So sorry to make this brief, but I need to end it before some nosy person comes along and spoils my chance." The man had made his way back to within a few feet of Mike, but when he struck this time Mike was ready for him. He watched the man's eyes and knew that he was going to fake to one side and strike toward the other trying to catch him off guard.

Mike parried the knife to the side and delivered a crushing blow to the man's sternum. He hadn't intended to land such a hard blow, but the man had fallen into the thrust when he had missed his target. Mike watched as it dawned on the man that his heart was no longer beating. The sudden shock had stopped it.

The man made a few gurgles and started to collapse. An older Asian man, dressed in traditional Chinese robes and probably headed for the market, had turned the corner just as the man landed at Mike's feet.

"Oh! Oh! What you do? Police, police!" The Asian man was making enough racket to wake the dead.

"Sir. Sir!" Mike needed to get the man's attention before he ran off.

The man stopped yelling when Mike didn't immediately run away. He calmed down even more when he finally stopped and really looked at the man on the ground. The knife was still in his hand. He took in the blood on Mike's shoulder and understood what had happened.

"You hurt much?"

Mike sighed, "I'm okay. Would you go to the market and call the police?"

"Ah! No need. Cell phone right here."

While the man called the police and explained in broken English where to come, Mike started doing his best to revive the man who had tried to kill him. He checked the man's heart to make sure that his heart was truly stopped before trying to do CPR. Thankfully, the new method for CPR didn't include the forced breaths. Mike wasn't sure he would go that far for the man. Why he should even try was just an indication of the type of man Mike was. He didn't wish to hurt anyone unnecessarily. Maybe the man deserved to die, but Mike didn't want to be the one to end his life. Beside the fact that he had questions he would like to ask. He needed to find out who hired him to kill him and why.

While Mike was performing CPR on his attacker a crowd had begun to form around him. The old Asian man had come back and had settled down across from him, watching his movements. Mike was too busy with his task to see that the old man had brought a plastic bag and had removed the knife from the attacker's hand, carefully placing it in the bag.

Sirens could be heard in the distance and within a minute two police cars were screeching to a stop close to the crowd, which quickly dispersed.

"What have we got?" The first policeman dropped down beside Mike and indicated the body lying on the street. A second policeman, Officer Blount according to his name tag, got on his radio and called in relaying the situation to their station and called for an ambulance to come to that address.

Since Mike was still trying to get the man's heart going and too busy to explain, the old Asian man told the police what he saw and gave them the knife that he had picked up and placed in the plastic bag.

The policeman crouched beside Mike gave him a funny look.

"You're trying to save the man who just tried to kill you?" Any criminal facing him would be intimidated just by his size and gruff voice. Mike took just a second to look up and answer, but the words caught in his throat. There was such a look of kindness in the policeman's eyes that Mike was taken aback just for a moment. It was at that same moment that the man lying at his feet took a deep shuddering breath and began to struggle.

The ambulance pulled up close to the crowd, and two EMTs hopped out and grabbed their gear. "Please, move out of the way. We need to get in here."

Officer Blount herded the few onlookers that were left out of the way and led the EMTs to the man on the ground. One of the EMTs took care of Mike's shoulder while the other EMT took the other man's vital signs.

"What happened to him?" The EMT looked to the officer for answers, checking the man over as he listened.

"This guy is fine, BPs a little elevated but that's it. He's going to have a pretty big bruise on his chest, maybe a cracked rib or two, but I'd say he's very lucky to be alive." He leveled an awed gaze on Mike. "That was one hefty punch. How'd you learn to do that? Is that some martial arts thing?"

Mike didn't give any response to the EMT's questions. He figured it was better that way.

One of the police officers rode in the ambulance with Mike's attacker, and another followed in one of the police cars. That left two police officers with Mike and the old man.

"Okay. Let's get a few questions answered." The large policeman with the kind eyes began the questioning.

"I'm Sergeant McClaskey and this is Officer Blount. First, tell me who you are." He directed the question to Mike.

"Sir, my name is Mike Calloway." He handed over his wallet with his White House identification in the front.

He looked over toward the Asian man.

"Chiang Chen." Mr. Chen bowed slightly toward the officer.

"Mr. Chen, I believe you are the one that called the police." At Mr. Chen's nod, the Sergeant went on. "Would you tell me what happened here, please?"

"I come 'round corner. Man fall at young man's feet. I call out for police. Then I see knife in man-on-ground's hand. Young man had blood on shoulder. I see bad man on ground, good man standing. He," pointing at Mike, "ask me to call 911. While I call police, young man proceed to save other man's life." He said that last part with what sounded like pride in his voice. He gave Mike a small bow and said no more.

"Okay. Thank you. Would you please come in to the station and give a statement? Officer Blount will give you directions."

"I know where is. My granddaughter dispatcher. I be there in morning." With that Sergeant McClaskey allowed the old man to go on his way.

"Good luck, young man," he said to Mike as he sauntered away toward the market with a smile on his weathered face.

"Well, let's go on down to the station so we can get this on tape. After you, Mr. Calloway." The Sergeant gestured to the back of the patrol car.

Ducking his head as he settled into the back seat, Mike couldn't help feeling a little like a criminal. He hadn't done anything wrong, but just sitting in the *back* of a police car made him feel that way.

Within minutes they were at the station and walking into one of the "conference" rooms. It was bare except for a table and a couple of chairs. They left him in there for just a few minutes and then they were back with an older woman, probably in her mid-forties. Nice looking, but she had such a stern look on her face it made her seem much older.

"Captain Calloway." She reached out to shake his hand. "My name is Captain Nielson. I am the station chief." She settled on the hard seat on the other side of the table from him.

"I will be taping your statement, if that's okay." She was being extremely gentle with him.

"Yes, that's fine."

She started the tape and filled in for the record who was taping the session, who Mike was, and the date and time.

"Good. Now, if you would begin and just tell what happened. Afterward I will ask you a few questions. If at any time you feel the need of a lawyer, just let us know.

A lawyer. But he hadn't done anything wrong. Mike was getting worried and his hands were getting clammy.

I will never leave you or forsake you.

Mike heard the statement almost as if God had spoken it straight into his ear. He calmed down immediately and began to tell how the man attacked him in the alley.

After he was finished, Captain Nielson asked, "The man said you had caused him a lot of trouble. What kind of trouble?"

"He said I should have died the first time."

"First time? You mean he has tried to kill you before? When was this?" Her eyes were wide in disbelief.

"I'm not sure, but I think he may have been the man who shot at the president's daughters."

"Wait, wait. What has that got to do with you… with this?"

"I'm one of the bodyguards for the president's daughters."

"Oh my God." She looked at someone standing behind Mike. "Get someone from the state department on the phone for me. I'll take it in my office." Officer Blount left to make the call.

"Young man, I'm sorry. I had no idea what I was dealing with here." She had turned the tape off moments before.

"I'll have to leave you while I take the call, but I'll have someone bring you a sandwich and something to drink shortly. I won't be long."

It was at least an hour before the station chief returned. When she did, her expression was grim and she didn't sit back down, opting to pace back and forth behind Mike's chair.

The door opened and two men in dark suits walked through the door. Captain Nielson came around the table to introduce herself and shake hands with Daniel Marlow, Head of Security for the White House, and the other security agent that accompanied him.

"Captain Nielson, thank you for calling us. We'll take over from here." With that firm dismissal, the Captain left Mike with the security men.

"Captain Calloway." Mr. Marlow reached out to shake Mike's hand. "I'm sorry you've been put through this. How about we get out of here to more favorable accommodations?" With that they walked out of the police station with Mike between them, causing heads to turn the whole way.

CHAPTER 40

In Horace Hadley's office the air almost crackled with the tension in the room. He was not just unhappy. He was beginning to be *scared* and that was something he hated. How had things gotten so fouled up? It shouldn't have been that hard to dispose of one insignificant man. Now he had another problem to get taken care of. Actually he had two problems. One was the man Meeker had hired to do the job. The other problem was Meeker. He was getting cold feet. The hold Horace had on him was not enough to overcome all the trouble this fiasco was causing.

"It's all your fault. If you hadn't killed that policeman ten years ago you wouldn't need to cover it up today." Meeker's voice was held low but it still scared Horace. This was his office.

"What if someone has bugged my office, you fool. Don't say anything about that. What's done is done."

"What are we going to do about it now? I'm out of answers." He looked like he had not had any sleep in a long time. There were dark circles under his eyes and his skin appeared loose and sallow. He didn't look well.

Hmm, Hadley thought, *maybe I can help that along.*

"Will your friend keep his mouth shut?" Horace stared at his campaign manager, looking for any sign of subterfuge.

"If he knows what's good for him, he won't answer any questions. He's very smart. I'm sure he has resources to help him get out before things go too far."

Horace wasn't sure at all. He didn't like loose ends and he was going to call someone to snip this loose end off, now, tonight. He waited for Meeker to leave before he called one of the goons he kept on retainer just for this sort of thing.

When the man answered, all Hadley said was, "Kill him," and hung up. He would dump the phone out the window as he passed over the Potomac River.

"What happened?" Marlow was yelling at the two guards that had been assigned to watch the man they believed shot at the president's daughters. They had been distracted for only a couple of seconds with a commotion down the hall from the man's room. Now the man they had learned was named Casio was dead. Shot right between the eyes with a silenced gun. They would get no more answers to their questions. Not one person saw or heard anything. They scoured the hospital and grounds but never found anything or anyone as a suspect.

It did give them some information besides the small amount they had gotten from this Casio when he did talk. Casio Lemaire was a known gun for hire. He had a long list of offenses, few for which he was ever prosecuted. He was always able, with high-powered lawyers, to beat the charges.

Now they knew that more was going on than what they had originally thought. This was a cover up attempt. Some of the things they were told by Casio Lemaire were going to be explosive when they came out in the media. It was unbelievable the names that were brought up. They were too late to cover it up. The main question the FBI didn't get answered was *why*?

Marlow loosened his tie. He had to call the president about all of this.

"Bob Meeker? Why in the world would Harold Hadley's campaign manager hire a man like this Lemaire to kill one of my daughter's bodyguards?" Cole was at a loss. He just couldn't believe the turn things had taken. Why? It just didn't make sense.

"What did he hope to accomplish?"

At the president's look, Marlow let out a deep sigh. "I'm not sure if we'll ever know, Mr. President. We got only a few answers from Lemaire, and those only after some very intense grilling. He said he didn't know the *whys*, just who to kill and how much money he would be paid by Meeker. He wasn't even sure if the money was coming from Meeker."

There was something in Marlow's voice. He either knew something or suspected something.

"Okay, Marlow, spill it. What are you holding back?"

"We've been kind of watching Meeker for a while now. We have reason to believe there is something he has done in the past that would stir up all kinds of trouble for him. Also," Marlow hesitated, "It could leave him open for blackmail if someone got their hands on the information."

"What kind of something? Espionage? Selling government secrets?" Cole shook his head at the thought. Meeker had never come across to him as a traitor type.

"More in the line of personal. We found a document. It could ruin his marriage and his reputation."

"Ah, yes. His revered marriage to his wife's inherited millions." Cole knew Meeker had married well. The only one who apparently didn't see that money was Meeker's real reason for marrying the quite heavyset heiress was Mrs. Meeker.

Cole took a stroll around his office. He loved this room, felt a belonging that would be hard to erase once his presidency was over. The room held so many secrets, some good, some bad. It seemed to have a living, breathing soul.

"Well, Daniel, have you spoken to Meeker?"

Marlow jumped at the President's question. It had been quiet for several minutes and Marlow's thoughts had drifted off to other responsibilities.

"Not yet, sir. We haven't been able to locate him. We are watching all the airports and bus terminals in case he tries to leave the country."

"What a mess. Keep trying to find him. He may be the only one who knows why all this was done. And I want him talking when you do find him."

Meeker would not be talking to anyone. He was found floating face down in one of the many hot tubs scattered over his palatial mansion two days later. A suspected heart attack, but it would be a hard job for the medical examiner to pin down because of the water and the temperature in the hot tub.

CHAPTER 41

Mike was determined to ask Randi out. How, he didn't know. She was so busy he hadn't been able to catch her for almost a week. Today, he found out from her brothers, she was leading the White House tours again. He was busy, too, escorting Brooke to the library. She had a couple of papers to write for school projects. So, after he got her settled in to study, he picked out a book on advanced engineering and sat on a comfortable sofa where he could see the other bodyguard at the door and see Brooke at all times. He let his mind drift to Randi, something that happened increasingly often. This last week he had missed seeing her. She didn't come by the apartment to see her brothers and he wondered if she was avoiding him. He thought they had established some kind of friendship while he was in the hospital. Maybe that was just kindness on her part and he was making too much out of it. That depressed him. He wanted it to be more, even more than just friendship. He wondered about Randi's parents. He knew they were well educated and both worked in the political setting. He knew her mother was an interpreter at the

White House and her father was an Ambassador to the United Nations. Would they think Mike didn't have much to offer their daughter? He never talked about how much money he had available were he to ever want to use it for anything. He hoped his career in the military would be enough to show he could provide for her. *Provide? Like in getting married?* He thought about that for a few minutes, and…yeah. He wanted to marry her.

Though Mike was deep in thought, as soon as Brooke closed her book, he was there beside her.

"Ready to go?" At her nod, Mike helped her pick up her papers and stuff them in her pack. Brooke walked toward the door where the other bodyguard stood while Mike called the driver to bring the car around.

"Did you get your reports done?" Always mindful of his duty, Mike slipped in front of her so he could check outside.

"Yeah. I'm finally done. Mom would be proud. I got them done and they aren't even due until Friday."

He chuckled at that. Typical teenager. He remembered back during his own schooling. Of course, his was so totally different from the norm. He was home schooled, but even that didn't quite describe how his schooling was. His parents had taken such an active role in teaching him. Allowing him to think things through before helping him. Then, challenging him to go further than just answering the question, they encouraged him to dig and find the reasoning behind the question. He was never chastised for a wrong answer. He just had to reason out where he had gone wrong, and then, find the right answer. If he still couldn't figure it out, then they would show him from the beginning.

When they were back in the car, Brooke looked over at Mike. Something was wrong. He'd been quieter than normal. Of course, he had been through a lot in the last few weeks. She wasn't a psychiatrist or anything but she bet it had to do with Randi. Would he tell her if she asked?

"Mike?"

"Umm? Everything okay?"

"Can I ask you a question? You don't have to answer if you don't want to."

He turned so he could see Brooke's face. He had never heard her so hesitant to speak her mind.

"Sure. What's on your mind?"

"Do you like Randi?" I mean like like."

He understood what she meant. He liked Randi more than just a friend *like*.

"Brooke…" She laid her hand on his arm and it seemed so natural for him to lace his fingers with hers.

"I know she really likes you. She kind of lights up when anyone talks about you."

That made Mike smile and gave him some hope that this thing between him and Randi wasn't all just in his imagination.

"Yeah, I like like her. A lot." He smiled as he said it and his heart felt lighter than it had in a long time.

"Mel, I...I can't tell you how sorry I am that they've started attacking you, too." He placed his hand on his friends' shoulder.

"Cole, we know each other well. I know and you know these pictures are fakes. The country knows it too. It's just too stupid to believe. Hadley pulled a real doozy this time and I believe it'll backfire on him. I really don't see anything to worry about. Actually, if you look at the polls, your rating went up just a notch. People know dirty politics when they see it, and they don't like it."

Cole scanned Mel's face. What he saw reassured him. He dropped his hand off his friend's shoulder after a slight squeeze.

"Okay, let's get on with the day. There is a lot to get done and a country to take care of."

He called his Chief of Staff in with the morning briefings and sat behind his desk ready to do the business of the office he held.

CHAPTER 42

"Okay, guys. Let's get things cleared out here." Will and Jeff had some of the older youth on a camping trip this time, in the mountains of Virginia, but now it was time to get them up and clear out all their trash and roll up their tents. Nothing would be left behind to spoil the beauty of the surroundings.

"Oh, yeah, Jim and Wally, you two are on latrine duty. Don't forget to cover everything up neatly. Right?" Jeff glanced over at the two boys for confirmation. They grimaced but each one gave the thumbs-up sign.

It had been such a good time for all of them. Two guys they had been praying hard over had really opened up about their problems. Some of the boys' home lives were pretty bad. Some didn't even want to go home because of what they had to put up with. A couple of the boys were in foster care. They were the lucky ones.

"Can't we stay another day?" Jim asked. He was one they fought hard to reach but had yet to get anywhere. Just him asking to stay longer showed promise.

"Sorry, but we have to get back tomorrow so we can get ready for Sunday. I expect to see you all there.

Okay?" Jeff heard a few good-natured grumbles but overall they said they would be there. He loved this job and he loved these kids. Young men really. They were mostly older teens right on the brink of manhood. What happened in the next couple of years could set the pattern for the rest of their lives.

"Hey, will your sister be there like last week?" This came from one of the oldest teens. Jeff and Will looked at each other. They knew Todd had a crush on Randi. Randi had come at their request to give a devotional for the guys and Todd couldn't keep his eyes off her. When she asked him a question, he froze and couldn't form an answer. None of the guys really picked at him because they were a little in awe of her, too.

"Not this week. Maybe some time soon, though." Will laughed at Todd's crestfallen look.

Randi couldn't seem to concentrate. It had been a week since she had seen Mike, but it seemed much longer. Today she was having lunch with DeeAnn.

They had been friends a long time and instead of drifting apart after high school they became even closer. The only thing Randi regretted was that she couldn't seem to break though this barrier that DeeAnn put up between herself and God. Oh, she said all the right things, and Randi thought DeeAnn's parents believed she was okay and had a relationship with the Lord, but Randi knew there was a part of DeeAnn that had not been surrendered to God's authority. There was a lack of trust on DeeAnn's part that hindered her from having that closeness Randi felt in her own life. Randi was pulled from her thoughts by the ringing of her phone.

DeeAnn called and said she would meet her at the Thai restaurant they both liked, the Bangkok One, but she might be a couple of minutes late. Charlie had been a little late picking her up and the traffic was terrible today. Randi looked at the time. She might be a few minutes late herself. She speeded up a little.

The limo pulled up close to the front door of the Thai restaurant just about five minutes late. Charlie jumped out to help DeeAnn from the car and sent the other bodyguard to open the door to the restaurant.

As DeeAnn scanned the restaurant for Randi, Charlie sent the car on and said to pick them up at one o'clock.

"Do you see Randi, Charlie?"

Charlie looked around the room, "Maybe she's just late…later than us."

"You think so? Let me call her." Randi's phone rang until it went to voicemail.

"Randi, are you close? We're here at the restaurant. Call me." Charlie guided DeeAnn to the table waiting for them. He sat down across from her facing the door so he could see anyone coming in.

What is this guy doing? Randi was trying to make her way to the restaurant but this guy kept getting in her way. He would pass her car and, all of a sudden, put on his brakes making her have to swerve to avoid a rear-end collision.

She finally made it around and was going to speed up a little to get further away from the man. She put her foot down a little harder, but before she could pull further away the big dark SUV behind sped up and rammed the rear of her car. She was so startled she almost lost control and hit the car beside her. The defensive driving her brothers had insisted on helped her keep it together until she could pull off where the shoulder of the road was wide enough to be safe.

Before she could get out to inspect the damage, her door was jerked open and the man who rammed her pulled her out.

"Stop it. Let me go!"

"Shut up. Now. Or I'll shut you up." Randi realized the man was pushing her toward his vehicle and knew she would be dead if he got her in there. She struggled even harder.

"Help! Help me!" Randi screamed, but no one was close enough to hear. Her screams abruptly stopped as the man hit her in the head with something hard, stunning her long enough to shove her in the back of the SUV. She kicked her foot at the man's head, hitting him on the right cheek with the heel of her shoe. The man swore and shoved Randi harder into the back of the vehicle. He cuffed her to a strap in the back then jumped in the driver's seat and took off. The whole scene had taken less than two minutes.

Randi pulled so hard at the handcuffs restraining her that her wrists began to bleed. "Why are you doing this? Please let me go. Just put me out right here." She tried to use a reasonable sounding voice, refusing to beg or get hysterical. The man just looked back at her and smirked.

Dear God, I need you to be with me. Please protect me and help someone find me soon. Her cell phone kept going off in her pocket but she couldn't get her hand down far enough to reach it. She looked toward the front of the van as she heard the man talking on his phone… about her. She listened to every word. If she got out of this, she wanted to be able to give the police as much information as she could. Her ears were tuned in to the man's voice, but her eyes were trained on the scenery that flew by the windows. If she could just get to her cell phone before he took it away, she could relay her whereabouts to the police or her family, someone. Her phone had been ringing when the man was ramming the rear of her car, but she couldn't let go of the wheel long enough to answer. Maybe DeeAnn was checking on her and would realize something was wrong. She tried to get her hip up to where her hands were cuffed, but it was impossible with the swaying car to get her hand in her pocket.

"Be still!" the man yelled.

"I have her. I'll put her where you said. Then I want my money." The man had called the number as he had been instructed, and now all he had to do was wait for the payoff…and what a payoff. Ten grand for one little lady.

Yeah, she was sure pretty, but that didn't excite him near as much as the money.

Randi couldn't figure out what was going on. The man didn't seem to want to do anything to her and she breathed a sigh of relief at that. He had just taken her from the back of the SUV and re-cuffed her to a drainpipe under a freestanding sink inside an old empty warehouse. He moved away to make a couple of calls and she tried to listen to every word, but he was speaking so low some words she couldn't make out. She tensed as he walked back toward her. She flinched as he reached toward her, and he gave a roar of laughter before digging in her pocket and pulling out her cell phone.

"Okay, girlie. You call your friend. Put it on speakerphone. Tell her something came up and you can't meet her today. Do it now and no funny business. Don't try to send any message to her. Got it? *Got it?*" He grabbed a hand full of her hair and pulled hard when she didn't answer.

"Got it." Randi growled the words through clenched teeth. She wondered how this man could know she was meeting someone. She quickly dialed the phone and when she heard DeeAnn's concerned voice she almost lost it. She took a steadying breath before answering. She had to send some kind of message to DeeAnn that the man couldn't possibly pick up on. She watched the man's face as she explained to DeeAnn that she wouldn't be meeting her for lunch. The man watched her expressions for any sign that she might be trying to relay a message to her friend.

"Okay, hon. You're sure everything's okay?" DeeAnn thought Randi didn't sound like herself. It must have been something bad.

Randi tried to lighten her voice when the man glared at her.

"Everything's okay. Just a little problem with my boyfriend. I'll call you tomorrow."

"Alright. If you need anything, let me know." DeeAnn shut her phone and went over to Charlie.

"Something's wrong. That was Randi. She's not going to meet us…said something came up with her *boyfriend*." She nodded as she saw Charlie's eyebrows rise. They both knew Randi didn't have a boyfriend. *Oh God, please, please let Randi be okay.* She tried to keep the tears back until the driver could get the car back to the restaurant but it was so hard.

Charlie called the other bodyguard, Rick, over and spoke to him quietly while they were waiting.

Randi's phone rang just after she ended the call with DeeAnn. The man took the phone from her and smashed it under his boot. He patted her face with his dirty hand, making her flinch. He just gave a bark of laughter.

"Don't want anyone tracking you. Do we, pretty girl?" The man pulled his own phone out and moved far enough away from her where she couldn't listen in before calling. This gave Randi time to really look at the man. He was fairly short but his bulk made up for

it. She looked at his arms for any identifying marks…
no tattoos showing but he had a long ugly scar that ran
from his left eye across his cheek to past his left ear. Part
of the lobe had been cut off. He was ugly, and it wasn't
just the scar. His skin was pitted and thick, sallow. He
looked Caucasian with maybe a little Indian. American
Indian. His teeth were stained and a few were missing.
His hair was dirty and his breath and body stank.

"I want my money. I did my part. Now you pay
up." The man was talking low but his voice carried
well enough for Randi to hear every word. She heard
enough to know he wasn't the boss. She wondered,
*Who, then, would want to kidnap her? It wasn't making
any sense. Of course, her father and mother were both in
fairly high-level government positions, not to mention her
relationship with the president's daughters. But she didn't
think this was about any of that.*

Hadley was nervous. It didn't take a genius to figure
out this man was going to give him trouble. He would
have him taken care of soon. He wasn't about to pay the
man. First, he needed to get a new untraceable phone
so he could call that young man who had caused him
all these problems. Mike Calloway…aka…Sean Harris.

His old *friend* Meeker, before his tragic, untimely
death, had found the old camera in the young man's
apartment. Of course, the old fool had almost gotten
himself caught by one of the other young men staying at the apartment. That would have been hard to

explain. What Meeker didn't find were any photos. Not the ones Horace needed. Maybe the young man had destroyed them? Maybe he didn't know what he had and just threw them away. Nevertheless, Hadley couldn't take the chance the photos would surface. This was too important. This was his *entire existence* at stake here, not just the presidency. He had no intention of spending the remainder of his life in prison.

CHAPTER 43

Mike had been in the middle of calling Randi when her phone all of a sudden went dead. Nothing. He tried again and got the same thing. Maybe her battery had gone out. He would just call DeeAnn. He knew they were having lunch together. Mike and two of the other bodyguards were with Brooke and Brooke needed some information about the history of the White House for a report. She figured instead of looking through all the books she would just ask the expert on the subject... Randi.

"What's wrong?" Brooke had come up beside him as he went to call DeeAnn.

"I think Randi's phone is dead. I'll call DeeAnn and get her to let Randi on."

"Hi, Mike. I'm glad you called. Have you heard from Randi?"

Something crawled across Mike's skin. He felt a dread sweep over him like he had during that last mission. Something was terribly wrong.

"N...no." He had to try twice before his voice would respond. "I thought you two were meeting for lunch."

"We were supposed to, but Randi called at the last minute and said she wouldn't be able to make it. Mike, when I asked her if everything was okay, she said everything was fine, just a little trouble with her *boyfriend*."

Mike's heart did a somersault. *Boyfriend? I can't... no, no. That's not...*

"Mike," DeeAnn answered his unasked question, "Randi doesn't have a boyfriend. Something's wrong."

"Hav...have you talked to any of her family, Jeff, Will?"

"Charlie checked with Dan. He hasn't heard from her and neither have her parents. He's trying to get in touch with Jeff and Will. They..."

"Right, they are at that youth camping trip in Virginia." Mike was so tense he jumped when his phone beeped for a waiting call.

"I have another call. Maybe it's Randi getting back with me." Mike switched the phone over to catch the incoming call.

"Randi?" Silence.

A mechanical sounding voice began, "Mr. Calloway. Do not hang up. Listen carefully or you will never see your pretty little friend again."

Mike breath whooshed out of his lungs and he felt lightheaded. "Please don't hurt her, please."

"She won't be hurt, unless you fail to cooperate. Do you understand?"

Mike shook his head then realized the man, or whoever it was, couldn't see that.

"I...I understand. What do you want?" He was concentrating so hard on hearing everything, any background noise, inflection of voice. He missed the first part of the man's words.

"Wait, p-please repeat that."

"Mr. Calloway, you must listen. Pull yourself together. I will not repeat this again."

"Right, okay, okay. I'm ready" Mike wiped the beads of sweat that had gathered on his forehead. What he was really doing was setting his phone to record every word said.

"You have something I want. You bring them to me and I will tell you where to find your little friend. Contact no one. Tell no one. Do I make myself clear?"

"What could I possibly have…"

"You have some pictures." There was a deep silence on the other end of his phone. "Mr. Calloway, do you know the pictures I'm referring to?"

Mike immediately thought of the pictures he had developed and put in the safety deposit box in Pasadena then moved to a bank in D.C. recently. They have to be the ones. He knew they were important. He just didn't know how much…until now.

"I don't know." He tried stalling for time, hoping something would crack in his memory. Something was there, just beyond his reach.

"Yes, you do know. I want them. Bring them and any copies and negatives you have. Take them to the National Mall Park…all the way to the back. You'll get further instructions and told where the girl is then. Be there at exactly six this evening. Failure to follow my instructions will lead to your little friend's death. Do I make myself clear?"

Mike tried to speak past the lump of fear in his throat, "Yes, yes. I...I understand."

Dan was pacing the floor when the FBI and Secret Service showed up. They had asked him to get a recent photograph of Randi and have it ready for them to send out to law enforcement officers and the TV stations.... *I can't believe...Randi...my sweet baby sister. Kidnapped. My God.* He knew it was always a possibility with such high profile parents, but they were always so careful. Well, apparently not careful enough. Dad and Mom would be here in a few minutes and he didn't know how to tell them their only daughter had been taken by who knew what kind of animal. Tears sprang to his eyes at what Randi could be going through at this moment. He had always been her protector, the oldest brother, but since Randi was all grown up now it was hard to be there all the time.

God, Randi needs you. Be with her. Help her feel your presence. Protect her. I know I can't always be there, but I know you are.

CHAPTER 44

"Charlie?" Rick, the other bodyguard with DeeAnn, moved closer, so he wouldn't be overheard. "We have everybody on it. I'll call Mike…"

"No. I'll call. He's going to be devastated if anything happens to her." Charlie dialed the number but got a busy signal.

After several tries he gave up and decided to go over there. First he had to see DeeAnn back to the safety of the White House. He was afraid she was going to fall apart on him, but she kept it together. He was proud of the strength she showed in this situation. He knew how close she and Randi were, like sisters.

After he left her with a promise he would call as soon as he found out anything, Charlie went to find Mike. He turned in the limo and left in his own vehicle. He drove as fast as he could in the heavy traffic, but it still took him almost thirty minutes to get to the apartment where Mike was staying.

"Mike. Mike!" Charlie banged on the door until a neighbor started complaining and threatening to call the police. A big, really big, burly man came out of his house next door to the apartment. All he had on was a pair of frayed shorts and the way the muscles bulged on his bare upper torso was an indication of the strength of the man. Not someone you want to get riled up.

"He ain't there. Took off in a big hurry about a half hour ago. Now git out of here and let me get some sleep."

Charlie got back in his car, wondering where to check now. He couldn't waste time just running around, but he had to do something. He pulled out his phone and tried Mike one more time.

"Charlie, I can't talk long," Mike began before Charlie interrupted.

"Mike, God, I'm glad you answered. Where are you?"

"I can't go into that right now…"

"Mike, listen, we think something is up with Randi."

"I know, Charlie, I was contacted."

"Contacted? By who? What did they say? Why did they contact you and not Randi's family? DeeAnn is so worried about her. Why didn't you contact the FBI?"

"Charlie. Stop a minute." Mike was almost to the bank now. He had to get there before the bank closed for the day. He had to get through to Charlie to keep this quiet. Randi's life depended on it.

"How many people know Randi is missing?"

"What? Dozens. DeeAnn, the president, the FBI, the Secret Service. Her parents and Dan. They haven't been able to get in touch with Will and Jeff yet." What was the deal? Surely Mike wasn't wanting to keep it quiet.

"Charlie. He said he would kill…" Mike's voice broke on the last word, showing the tremendous emotional upheaval Mike had been going through.

"Who, Mike? Who is he and what does he want? Let us help. This is too big for one person to handle. Let the FBI and Secret Service do their jobs."

Mike hesitated. He knew he had to trust them. He, for sure, couldn't trust the man on the phone. He might take the pictures and never reveal where Randi was. Mike refused to think that Randi might already be dead. He couldn't accept that.

"Charlie, tell the FBI that I have gone to pick up some pictures."

"Pictures?! What…"

"He said I had to get the pictures and any copies and negatives. I was to bring them to the far edge of the park. After I get there he'll call with further instructions." Mike swiped at the tears that had gathered in his eyes.

Charlie was trying to understand what it was that Mike *wasn't* telling him.

"What do these pictures have to do with Randi?"

"I don't think they do."

"Mike, I don't understand. Just tell me what the pictures are about."

"I…Charlie, I don't know what they're about. Wait." Mike stopped Charlie before he could ask the question. He knew it was a weird story.

"Charlie, I have to get in the bank before they close, so I have to hang up. Get to the FBI office. I will copy and e-mail the pictures there. Find out who the man in the pictures is. I took the pictures ten years ago. The man is using Randi to get me to give him the pictures. I can't let anything happen to her. You understand that, don't you?"

"Of course, Mike. Don't do anything crazy. Okay? We're going to figure this out and get her back." Charlie closed his phone and rested his head on the steering wheel. "God, Mike and Randi are in trouble. Help us get them through this." Charlie had been in a similar situation some years before. It ended badly and someone he cared about had died. He would never forgive himself for not taking care of her, protecting her.

Randi couldn't feel her legs. She'd been sitting in an awkward position for what seemed like days, but must have been only couple of hours. The warehouse was shadowed, but it was not completely dark yet. She wished she knew what was happening. Why was this happening? The man that put her in this building had made a couple of calls and just left her here. In some ways she hoped he came back. Mostly she hoped she never saw him again for as long as she lived, which might not be all that long if someone didn't find her. She felt a tear slide down her cheek and tried to wipe it off against her shoulder. She would not break down. *Focus, Randi. Stop your whimpering and focus on getting out of here.*

Taking a deep breath, Randi looked around. It was getting darker. What was close to her that she could use? She scanned the area that she could see, turned her body around to look behind her, even though the movement made pain shoot through her wrists. Nothing, absolutely, nothing. Just filthy concrete and a few bugs, thankfully dead.

She had pulled on the handcuffs until her wrists were in terrible shape, blood running down her forearms. Looking at her wrists, she noticed how the pipe attached to the sink. Did it look just a little loose, right where it met the bottom of the sink? Stretching her hands apart as far as she could, she kicked with her heel toward where the pipe connected to the bottom of the sink. A lucky-placed kick knocked the pipe a little bit looser. Randi tried to pull on the pipe but it hurt her wrists too much. Another kick missed the pipe altogether, scraping her shin on the bottom edge of the sink and sending shockwaves through her wrists. The pain in her wrists and now her leg made her almost give up fighting to get loose. Anger at the man that did this to her gave her added strength on the next kick. When the pipe came loose, Randi's weight shifted and her head hit the edge of the sink, almost knocking her out. She sat for a minute trying to let the blackness fade. When she opened her eyes, she saw that the pipe had shifted just a little more, but maybe it would be enough. She was elated as she worked the cuffs up and was able to squeeze them through the break in the pipe. Her hands were still cuffed together, but she was free to move around at last. Her legs gave way when she tried to stand up, scraping her knees on the concrete floor.

Giving herself a minute to get feeling back in her legs, Randi scanned the room for a way out. Large double doors at either end. Padlock on one set. She eased to a standing position. Confident her legs would hold her up now, she went to the other set of doors. No padlock. She tried to pull the doors open. No such luck. She tried pushing them instead, but they wouldn't give an inch. There were lots of windows, all about fifteen feet up, and nothing for her to stand on. She was trapped here. Trying to push down a feeling of panic, Randi went to the Lord.

Father, I'm afraid. If there is a way to get out of here, please show me. Or send someone to help me. If I'm not meant to make it out, please be with my family. Comfort them.

"Have you seen these pictures? Could they be fakes? You know what Hadley did to President Harris and his family with those faked photos. Could this be retaliation?" Josh, the Secret Service Director, asked the group collected in his office. The Director of the FBI, Garrett Sullivan, looked at Charlie for an answer.

Charlie jumped out of the chair he had just sat down in. "I told you. I talked to Mike Calloway about them. He said he took them about ten years ago. He didn't know who was in the pictures. I could tell by his voice he didn't have a clue that it was Horace Hadley." He could tell both men were skeptical.

"Why did he have them in a safety deposit box?" Josh didn't like any of this. It all screamed set-up. He called one of his agents over and spoke in a low voice. "Check Calloway out. Finances, everything."

Charlie heard the soft words. "You're crazy if you think Mike is running a scam. You just had him checked out. He's just been vetted up one side and down the other in order to be a bodyguard for Brooke Harris. Did you not do a good enough job the first time?"

Josh scowled at him. "That's enough, Charlie. We just need to be very careful to do everything right. We can't have anyone saying the president had anything to do with this."

"So you are going to throw Mike under the bus?" Charlie looked at both men. "You just remember that Mike risked his life for that same president's daughters. He's one of the best men we have on the team." With that he walked out and slammed the door behind him.

"Josh, you know he's right." Garrett Sullivan stood up and walked out of the office.

Mike kept scanning the pictures in his hand. What was it about this man? Oh, it was easy to see why the pictures were explosive. The man was about to shoot another man in the head in one, and in another the man was no longer kneeling on the ground but was in a crumpled heap. But who was this man pointing the gun and why did he look so familiar? He hoped the FBI would be able to answer these questions quickly. He needed to find Randi before anything happened to her. He knew that the FBI, Secret Service, and law enforcement were looking for her. They were listening to any and all Internet chatter, checking out any old warehouses by using infrared scanners. They had helicopters everywhere. He just hoped the pictures he sent them helped narrow down who might be responsible. If they knew *who*, then maybe they could figure out *where* they had Randi.

He arrived at the park in record time. Out of the corner of his eye he saw a slight movement. A man was hidden in the trees to his left. He didn't know if this was his contact or someone else. He started to turn to his left when someone close by said, "Just keep walking, Mike. We have you under surveillance. Don't give our positions away." It was Rick's voice. Mike didn't know much about Rick's background, but he knew him to be a dedicated agent. Very well trained and good at his job. It made Mike feel better about the situation just having him there.

At the far end of the park, a short man with scrawny arms and legs waited for his mark to show up. He'd been given a photo of the young man to go by. If he didn't show up soon, he'd leave. It wasn't worth getting caught, even for all that money. Of course, all he had to do was get the pictures, check them over, and then kill the man that brought them. He had his gun ready, silencer in place. "Come on. I can't wait all day." The mosquitos were feasting on his skin in droves and he was sure some of them had to be carrying diseases.

The man didn't realize that he was under surveillance as well. One of the Secret Service agents, a seasoned super sleuth, code-named Tiger, had come in at the back of the park, slowly, so as not to spook anyone. He was the best at moving without being seen. Once he found the man's hiding place he had whispered the location to the other agents through his wrist microphone.

"We're coming your way, Tiger." Charlie pulled Mike to the side into the bushes where he had been following his movements. Mike was surprised to be stopped like that.

"Charlie, the man might see you," Mike protested.

"It's okay, Mike. We got him under watch. He's at the back of the park. We need to fit you with an earpiece so you can hear what's going on." As Mike started to protest, Charlie assured him the man would not be able to see the gadget. It was way too small and fit down inside his ear.

"Okay, you ready? Can you hear me?" Charlie had spoken softly into his wrist piece, and when Mike nodded, he directed him to move back into the lane. "Okay, guys, we're back on the move, coming your way."

The little scrawny man was about to head back out of the park the way he came in. Apparently the guy with the pictures wasn't going to show up. He had just started to turn his back on the open lane when he saw someone coming. He moved a little further into the bushes until he could see if this was his guy.

Mike kept his eyes trained ahead. He walked and prayed. He was almost at the back of the park. There the lane was a little wider making a bit of a clearing. As he stepped into the wider space, a small built man stepped out of the bushes almost right in front of him, making him jerk back.

"Stop where you are and let me see your hands." The man pulled a gun from inside his jacket and aimed it toward Mike's chest.

"The man is armed. Repeat, the man is armed," Mike heard through his earpiece.

"It's okay." Mike hoped the men watching him knew he was talking to them. "I'm not armed. I have what you're after. Please just tell me where Randi is."

"Don't know and don't care. I'm just here to pick up the package. Hand it over." He motioned with the gun.

"No, I want to know that Randi is safe before I give you this." Mike had a bad feeling that this man was telling the truth. He didn't know where Randi was. He was just being paid to get the package. Someone else was calling the shots.

"Who paid you to do this? I'll give the package to him, and only him. Call him. Now!"

"Who made you boss? You don't see this gun in my hand? That makes me boss. I call the shots." The little man almost giggled with glee.

"I don't think so. Look around." As the man looked around at the bushes surrounding them, men, with guns trained on *him* came out from everywhere. There had to be twenty men, all dressed in tactical gear and all looking angrily at him. The hand holding the gun shook so much he almost dropped it. He knew he was in trouble. The money meant nothing to him if he was dead, and he knew if he even moved a hair, he would be dead before he hit the ground.

"C-c-can we talk about this." He felt the rivulets of sweat run down his face and armpits.

"Drop the gun gently and take two steps back, no more," Tiger instructed from behind him. The voice was soft, but it sent shivers of fear down the little man's back.

The man dropped the gun and took two shaky steps back. He wanted so badly to turn and run, but he knew better than to do that.

"Mike." Charlie gave Mike the go ahead to question the man.

"Where is Randi?"

The man swallowed at the hard lump in his throat. "I-I truly don't know. I wasn't told about any Randi. I was just hired to-to take the package and k-kill the man who brought it."

"Who contacted you?"

"I d-don't know. I do an Internet site. People text me. I never know who."

Mike could feel panic setting in. How was he going to find Randi? Was she okay? Surely they would have contacted him if she had been found. He could feel despair setting in. Would he ever see Randi again... *alive?*

"You said Internet site. Do you do this through your phone?"

"Y-yes." He knew what was coming.

"Is that how you will be contacted to get the money?" Mike had stepped closer to the man so he could judge his reactions.

"Yes. Whoever it is will send the money to my account after I tell him the job is done and put the package where I've been instructed."

"Get his phone and empty his pockets," Charlie instructed one of the agents. "You," he pointed at the scrawny man, "call or text this person. Let them know you've done the job and want your money. Where were you supposed to put the package?" The man hesitated for just a moment, but realized he had no bargaining chips to help him out of this.

"There is a maintenance room on the fourth floor of the Hyatt Regency on Capitol Hill. I was supposed to put it behind a case of those long fluorescent light bulbs." The man's Adam's apple bobbed as he tried to swallow.

CHAPTER 45

Randi made the rounds inside the building again and again, searching for something, anything she could use to pry open one of the doors. She kept wondering. *Why. Why am I here? Are they coming back to do something to me? Will I ever see Mike again?* She sat down on the cold floor and started to cry. She didn't want to cry. She wanted to be angry, and she was, but the tears continued to seep out. Tears for a life cut short, for relationships that would never happen, for the children she would never have. She thought about Mike and what their children would have looked like. A handsome little boy with his daddy's eyes, a pretty little blonde girl with her daddy wrapped around her little finger. She wanted that, more, she realized, than any career, any ambassadorship. She wanted Mike in her life.

"God, if this is a test, I know I'm failing miserably. Please give me the strength to face whatever comes without fear."

Was that a noise? She rose from the floor where she must have fallen asleep. Yes! It was a noise. Fear rose up in her throat. No, God is with me. I will not fear them or what they do. A loud noise at the door made her jump.

She backed away from the door just as it flew open. Men in black uniforms piled into the room with guns drawn. She backed as far away as she could with her back against the far wall.

"Ma'am, are you alone?" One of the men came closer to her. He didn't look threatening and Randi began to hope.

"Yes. I'm alone."

"Are you hurt anywhere?" He came closer and she could tell he was part of the SWAT team by the emblem on his vest.

"I'm okay. So much better now that you're here. Do you know who did this? Who put me here? How did you find me?" All the questions just seemed to barrel out of her.

"I'm sorry, ma'am, I can't answer your questions just yet. Let's get you to the hospital to be checked out. Then someone will meet with you for a statement." His voice was so kind and soothing she calmed down immediately.

"Sue," he called to a young woman in tactical gear. "Get these cuffs off her, okay? Then help her to the ambulance." He didn't know what she had been through so he didn't want to get too close and frighten her. He figured a woman agent would be less of a threat.

"Yes, sir. I'm on it." As Sue came toward Randi to take off the cuffs, Randi held out her arms.

"Wow. Let's get you in that ambulance so they can take care of those wrists." Sue shook her head. The girl had really fought those restraints.

"We have the girl. She's okay. Taking her to be checked out at George Washington Hospital." The SWAT team leader called in the report to the Head of Security at the White House as instructed. He looked over at the girl. She seemed to be okay, a little nervous but under the circumstances he had expected to find her screaming and in tears. Instead she walked calmly with Sue toward the open door and followed him to the car and got in. Plucky. And, whew, gorgeous to boot.

"Mike. They found Randi. She's okay. Nod if you heard me." Charlie's voice shook as he said the words. He knew how much it meant to Mike.

Mike wanted to shout praises to the heavens, but instead he just nodded as Charlie had said. He could do nothing about the huge grin that formed on his face.

"Thank you, God. Thank you so much," he whispered. He wanted to see her, make sure she was truly okay, but right now he had a mission to accomplish.

CHAPTER 46

Trouble. He was in so much trouble. Horace brushed a hand through his ever-thinning hair. As he shifted in his chair in order to look past the boldly striped curtains of his office window, he wondered how to fix this situation. He should have known not to trust that scrawny little creep to do the job without getting caught. At least he had made sure no one could connect him to Horace. The computer access he had used had been stolen from someone that couldn't be connected to Horace in any way and the computer was stolen as well.

He had been keeping an ear out for any word about the girl. Now they had found her. He couldn't imagine how they had located her so fast. He had expected to have at least a few days before they found her. With that Harris boy dead, Horace should have been home free. Things didn't turn out the way he had hoped, but he had other plans already in the works. He was a survivor, but he survived because he always planned ahead.

The guy he hired to kidnap her was taken care of. That was good. He hadn't talked to anyone, and now he never would. Did that mean they had captured the little creep who was bringing him the pictures? Well, he would have to do something. His fingers started dialing his office phone before he realized what he was doing.

No…can't use that phone. He shivered at the mistake he had almost made. He took out the throw away phone he kept for these occasions and dialed his most trusted (if there was such a thing) employee.

"Coker, I need you to fix something." He told the man what he wanted done then hung up the phone. There was no discussion of fees or any question that the job would be done. That was all prearranged, just the timing was a little earlier than expected.

Randi was okay. She was safe. Dan almost broke down at the news. Word had come through from Charlie that the Federal SWAT team leader, Camden Calloway, was taking her to the hospital just to be checked out and they could meet them there. Dan and his parents hugged each other at the news and bowed in a prayer of thanks that Randi had been found and was not harmed. Jeff and Will were on their way back from their camping trip. They had already been packed up to leave before they got word about Randi being missing, but got into a traffic jam on the freeway that had tied them up for several hours.

"Will, it's Dan. Randi's been found. She's okay." The whoops of joy pounded his eardrums. "Meet us at the hospital. No, no. It's standard procedure, just to check her out. Make sure she's as okay as she seems."

He could hear Will explaining things to Jeff. They were such good guys, wonderful brothers. He was so proud of them. They said they would meet him at the hospital, so Dan left with his parents to be at the hospital as soon as they could. He didn't want Randi alone even for a moment.

"That's wonderful news. I know your family was so worried. So were Celeste and I." The Raes had been friends of theirs for years. Cole remembered watching DeeAnn and Randi as they grew up together. He was aware how much Randi had helped his daughter to adjust to life in the White House, how much a friend she had been to DeeAnn. DeeAnn hadn't stopped crying since Randi had gone missing. Now she was on her way, with her escorts, to see Randi when they finally got her to the hospital. He imagined it would be standing room only what with all the family and friends, plus all the media and security people.

Tully and Carmen Rae fought down the tears the President's words evoked. Cole and Celeste were two of the best people one would ever want to meet. They had been friends of the Raes for many years and with Cole becoming President it didn't change them like it had so many others. The Harris's were the same down-to-earth people they had always been. DeeAnn had been at their home so much she was almost like a second daughter. Jeff and Will had certainly treated her that way, always picking at her the same as they did Randi, but always protective as well. Lately, though, Carmen had sensed a tension between DeeAnn and Jeff. When she asked Jeff, he had just shrugged it off as nothing.

CHAPTER 47

"Mike. We're gonna have to let the guy do this. He has to put the package there himself in case someone is watching. And I'd bet my next paycheck someone will be." Charlie knew Mike didn't want to let the man go free in case they lost him. It was a tough decision but they couldn't think of any other way to handle it.

"I guess so. Just make sure someone is close enough to grab him. Okay? I want to catch the man who did this to Randi."

They were in the office of the Head of Security for the White House. Garrett Sullivan had ordered them some coffee and then had to leave to take care of some security at the hospital for Randi. Josh had left them there to make some calls, but when he returned all of them would finalize plans for the drop.

"Where is the man…what was his name?" Mike looked over as Rick pulled out the wallet that he had taken from the man in the park.

"Would you believe this?" Rick hooted with laughter. "The man's name is Percy Peeves." Not a name one would think of as a hardened criminal. "Look at this.

He's got a wife? Three kids?" Rick whistled softly and handed the photo over to Charlie who looked at it briefly and passed it on to Mike.

"Why would a man, with what looks like a nice family, get involved in something like this?" Mike just shook his head. This woman and her children were the ones who were going to suffer. By morning it would be all over the news and their names would be dragged through the mud. The picture looked to be a few years old going by how the man looked now. The children, two boys and a girl, were teenagers in the picture. The boys looked like their dad, small built and not much on the looks department, but the girl took after her mother. She had long black hair that hung in a mass of curls down her back, and her eyes were an opalescent grey. Unusual eyes. The mother wasn't the stunner that the girl was but she was a good-looking woman. Mike glanced up as Josh Key strode back into the room. He didn't know why, but, instead of handing the photo back to Rick to put in the man's wallet, he slipped it into his own shirt pocket.

"Okay, everyone. Show's on." He filled them in on how things would unfold. A lot of planning had taken place in a very short time, but there were so many angles to cover. They couldn't take a chance on anything going wrong, so they coordinated their plans with the FBI and the SWAT team that had been involved earlier. The police were keyed in on what was going down and would help with the surveillance. They helped plan the route Mr. Peeves would travel and Josh designated agents and officers to watch any and all side roads. They checked all roads leading from the Hyatt Regency and placed officers there as well.

Mike rode down in the elevator with Charlie, Rick, and Josh Key. His mind was in a whirl. He wanted so badly to be with Randi at the hospital, but he knew catching who did this had to be his priority. He caught Charlie glancing at him from time to time. He knew they were worried that he wouldn't be able to keep it together when he confronted the man.

"It's okay, you know. I'm not going to go off the deep end. Now if anything had happened to Randi…" He left the rest unsaid, but Charlie and Rick could imagine what Mike meant. They had a feeling Mike could be lethal if he chose to.

As the elevator stopped, Josh let the other two men exit ahead of him. He scanned the parking area for the van that would carry them to the drop site. It was just easing into a parking space at the end of the lot. The van was white, of course, and non-descript. No government or police markings.

"Ready?" Josh gave a circular motion with his hand, and the van pulled down and opened its side door to let the three men enter.

CHAPTER 48

"Randi? Are you sure you're okay?" DeeAnn had asked her at least a dozen times. They were in her hospital room. The door was closed, but Randi knew there were two big, armed, Secret Service agents just outside her door. There was also a SWAT team member stationed close to the front doors of the hospital, and one at the ER entrance, according to Dan. He and her parents had just left to get something to eat. Her mother was going to spend the night with her despite Randi's assurances that it wasn't necessary. The sterile room was making her jittery. Or, just maybe, the fact that she'd yet to see Mike. She had a revelation about her feelings for Mike during this time, but maybe Mike didn't feel the same way. Maybe he was just being friendly because of Jeff and Will.

"He'll be here, honey. He just has some things to take care of." DeeAnn had read her thoughts, as usual.

A knock on the door brought her head around to see her two brothers as they peeked in. She knew they had had to go through all the security in order to get this far. Especially since DeeAnn was in the room. But their names were on a short list of acceptable people to allow through.

"Hey, guys. Come on in." For some reason DeeAnn decided she had to go right then. Some appointment that she had almost forgotten. She hugged Randi and said a quick goodbye to Jeff and Will before escaping out the door.

Jeff just shrugged his shoulders. She just wouldn't stay near him long enough for him to even talk to her. *What did she have against him?*

Randi saw it bothered Jeff a lot that DeeAnn had taken off so quickly. Maybe she should talk to DeeAnn about it, try to get her to open up.

"Hey, you two. How was your trip?"

Jeff gave her an *are you kidding* look, then answered her question with one of his own. "And how are you today? Oh, what's this? You're in the hospital?"

"Okay, okay, very funny. I'm fine, guys." She took each one by the hand. "I had a lot of people praying for me. I wasn't hurt." She caught them looking at the bandages around each wrist.

"I did that to myself trying to get loose," she explained.

Jeff leaned over her bed, still holding her hand tightly, "You weren't hurt any other way?"

Randi knew what they were asking her and she was glad that she could reassure them on that. "No. He didn't try anything like that. Other than shoving me in the van and forcing me into that building, he didn't hurt me. I think he was only interested in the money he was going to be paid."

DeeAnn had to get out of the room as soon as Jeff got in there. She didn't know what it was about him that made her so uncomfortable. She knew how dedicated he was to Randi. He was a great guy according to everyone that knew him. In his tan chinos and white pullover he was devastatingly handsome. He was a Youth Director at his church. A very moral, religious man. Maybe that was the problem. She went to church and her family was very religious, not just for show, but they had deep convictions about God. She just never had gotten into the whole religion/God thing. She felt this extreme attraction whenever she was around Jeff, but she knew they were just not suited for each other. She didn't measure up to his high standards. She could feel the tears start to well up in her eyes, and she tried to steel herself against them. *Don't cry. Don't cry.* At last she made it out to the car with her bodyguards beside her all the way. At least Charlie wasn't there. He was still tied up with the kidnapper situation. If he saw her right now, he would know something was wrong and wouldn't hesitate to ask about it. She couldn't talk to him about it. She knew only too well that Charlie had feelings for her and as much as she liked Charlie and trusted him, she just didn't have those same feelings for him. Not like she did toward Jeff. There! She admitted she had feelings for Jeff. Not that it would do any good. He was too good for her. He needed someone who could work alongside him in his church work and she just couldn't be that person.

CHAPTER 49

Mike and Charlie were at the SWAT team's headquarters at Quantico with the men who would escort Mr. Peeves to the drop site. Mr. Peeves was being held at a location not too far from the Hyatt. A whole crew of police and SWAT team members were already taking their places along the route Peeves would travel and at the Hyatt Regency Hotel. They were leaving nothing to chance. They had to make sure whoever picked up the pictures was apprehended. Was it possible that person might be Horace Hadley, candidate for the presidency? Maybe it was someone wanting to blackmail him. There was plenty of evidence to do just that. This was explosive stuff.

Mike couldn't be still. He was worried about Randi. He had heard that she was okay, but he still hadn't talked to her. He wanted this to be over with, only he knew when all of this was revealed to the public it was going to cause problems with the election. He wasn't sure how the government would handle it.

"Mike," Charlie motioned him over so they could talk privately.

"Charlie, what is it?" Mike could tell whatever it was he wasn't going to like it.

"Mike. You gotta stay here and wait for us." Charlie waited for Mike's reaction and it wasn't long in coming.

"No way! This is something I need to do, Charlie. Surely you understand that. He kidnapped Randi. Besides, I took those pictures. They're mine." He shook Charlie's hand off his shoulder.

"I know how you feel. I really do. I'd feel the same way. But, Mike, it's because of those things that you can't be involved in the takedown. Think about it for a minute." Charlie watched as Mike processed all he had said and knew he was going to do the right thing. "I promise I'll keep you up to date on everything that goes down."

Mike hated it, but Charlie was right. He was too much a part of what was happening. It could cause problems in getting a conviction against Peeves as well as hamper the investigation into Hadley's part in what happened in the photos.

"I want an earpiece. I want to know what's taking place."

Charlie smiled, "I bet I can get that okayed."

While they were getting Mike fixed up again to listen in to the takedown, the SWAT team was getting Peeves ready and informed on the route he had to go.

The SWAT team was ready. Peeves was being escorted to the basement where his dark blue Volvo was hidden in the parking garage. A GPS had been placed in his car just in case something went wrong. Peeves had the photos and his cell phone. Of course his cell phone was being monitored constantly so he couldn't call to warn anyone. The only call he should be making was after he placed the package and then he would call for his money to be sent. A Secret Service agent could hear everything said on both sides and would feed Peeves the words to say. When the money was transferred, a tech guru would follow that transmission back not just to a phone but also to the exact location of the phone. Hopefully.

"Let's get this done. Don't do anything foolish, Mr. Peeves," the voice said in his ear.

Percy's hands were slick on the steering wheel and he felt nauseated with fear. A cold sweat was running down the sides of his face. His shirt was plastered to his back, making him stick to the back of the seat.

How was he ever going to get out of this? He started the car, grinding the starter in his nervousness, and pulled slowly forward out of the parking garage. His mind was whirling. Maybe he could veer off the route they told him to go. If he just went down…no. He was sure they would have every exit watched. If he didn't do exactly as he was supposed to, they would pick him up and throw him so far into prison no one would ever find him again. Probably put him somewhere as a terrorist or something.

Charlie and Rick, along with the Federal SWAT team traveled the forty or so miles from Quantico to where Peeves was being held at the FBI field office on 4th Street. From there they would shadow Peeves' car down 4th Street to New Jersey Avenue straight to the Hyatt Regency.

Charlie was hyped. This was the biggest thing he had been involved with in his career. He realized it could get really ugly if Hadley was cornered, but they would deal with that when the time came. Personally, he hoped Hadley would have the sense to give himself up. He had to know he would never get out of this. His career was ruined and he had done it to himself. He just hoped no one got hurt.

"Mike. We're meeting up with Peeves' car as it comes out of the FBI Field Office parking garage right now. We're on our way!"

"Mike was listening to everything as it happened. It wasn't the same as being there, but he understood why he couldn't be. He said a silent prayer for all the men and women involved – that they would be safe. He even said a prayer for Horace Hadley. He didn't know what made a man do the things Hadley had done, but he was a human being and he needed prayer probably more than anyone else.

As Mike listened in, he could tell they were getting close to the hotel. The chatter went up more as they closed in around the building, trying to remain as unnoticeable as possible. Josh Key would be the one to go in the hotel and inform the manager that the building was in lock-down. No one in no one out unless it was Hadley. All the officers had been informed to remain hidden if they saw Hadley approach the building. Right now they were just supposed to watch the entrances until Peeves placed the package and made the call.

Peeves was on route just a couple of blocks from the hotel when his phone rang. It was Hadley. Peeves lied when he said he didn't know who was behind the kidnapping. Though even Hadley didn't know that Peeves knew. Peeves had resources of his own and those resources had led him straight to Hadley's identity. Percy Peeves was no fool. He wouldn't work blindly for any amount of money.

He got the okay from the voice to take the call and pressed the button for talk.

"Where are you? Do you have the package?" Hadley's voice sounded strange, muffled.

"Yeah. I got it. I'm just a couple of blocks away."

"He gave you the package even though they found the girl?" Hadley asked suspiciously.

The voice in his ear prompted him, "Tell him you got the package and got away, no problem. You don't know about any girl."

Peeves did as he was told. He wasn't sure Hadley believed him though.

"Put the package where I told you and then call me. I'll make sure you get paid."

He wanted to get out of this alive. He also wanted to make a deal that he wouldn't be prosecuted given his cooperation in making the drop, but he didn't think they were going to go for that. He would probably spend time in prison. He knew his wife would leave him. He couldn't understand how such a lovely woman had agreed to be his wife. He had felt truly blessed, so why had he done this stupid thing? He wanted the money. Money he could use to shower her with all the things she deserved. She had given him three beautiful children, even though each pregnancy had been terribly hard on her. She was an amazing woman. Now he had probably lost her as well as his sons and daughter. They would lose all respect for him.

Hadley didn't wait any longer. He wanted to have time to slip out before things got any hotter. He was on the second floor in a room he had rented two weeks ago under an alias. An identity he had made up several years back. He had a credit history, an extensive bank account, and a passport all under this cover name. If he couldn't pull this off, he would just disappear and resurface as this business tycoon. He might need to change his appearance some, but that would be for the better anyway. No one was going to keep him down for long. He would just reinvent himself. It could be done. People did it all the time.

He pulled a second phone from his pocket and dialed the number that would end all his problems.

Peeves heard a phone ringing somewhere. It wasn't the one in his hand. What phone was it? Where was it?

That was the last thought he had on this earth as the blast from under his seat tore through his body, sending pieces of it and his car flying off in all directions.

The explosion almost deafened the agents listening in. All they could do was watch as Peeves' car – what was left of it – flattened a streetlamp and careened into a concrete bench. A number of people had to dodge out of the way or be run over. Someone called 911 and a couple of people gathered near to see if they could help the driver, but quickly realized that no one could still be alive in that car. Some people gathered around the car at a safe distance where they could watch. Mothers steered their young children away from the site of the wreckage. Josh and Charlie watched from the white van as the car belched fire and the wheels caught on fire, filling the avenue with billows of black smoke.

"He either knew we had Peeves bugged, or he was just being extremely cautious. Maybe he didn't care about getting the photos. He just didn't want them surfacing." Josh didn't really care which it was. He was just so stomping mad that things had gone the way they had.

"Charlie, check in with the agents at the exits. See if anyone tried to leave. Check with the manager. I want the names of every person who rented a room for the last two weeks checked out. I want to know who they are, where they are, and what they look like. Get footage from all cameras in the area. I want to know who came anywhere near here in the last two weeks."

Rick broke in to their conversation, "I called the bomb techs. They're on their way."

Josh shook his head. What a mess. Surely Hadley didn't think he could get away with all this. They had enough evidence to put him away forever.

CHAPTER 50

Horace Hadley had already left the hotel. He had walked out the side entrance and no one gave him a second look. As he made his way down the street, he tugged at the maid's outfit that kept riding up in the back. It wasn't very comfortable, but it would do for now. He laughed a little at his reflection in one of the store windows. Made a pretty good-looking woman, if he did say so himself. If he could just make it back to his office undetected, he would have a perfectly good alibi. *They may think they have me but they can't prove anything now.* He laughed a little to himself, causing a few people to stare at him, something he absolutely didn't want.

"We have him, Josh. All we gotta do is send the team and pick him up. He thinks he made it safely back to his office, but we got him on tape. A little weird looking in the maid outfit, but we have face recognition…it's him. He changed clothes and left for his apartment."

Garrett Sullivan scanned the room. All his top agents were there. They had congregated at the FBI Field Office to discuss how to proceed with the take down.

Styrofoam cups were on every available space. Coffee had flowed freely until the wee hours of the morning. They were all tired but hyped. In the early hours of this morning they would hit Hadley's apartment. They had allowed him to think he had gotten away, back to his office undetected. Of course, they had people watching his every move. They had followed him back to his apartment and he had stayed there. No one came in and no one came out.

Storming Hadley's apartment was set for six this morning. He needed the guys to go and get a couple of hours shut-eye. He wanted them alert when this thing went down. No goof-ups. They were going to be grilled about everything they did and it had to be perfect and documented.

Mike had taken off as soon as he could to the hospital to see Randi. He was expected to be back at five so he could listen in during the arrest of Hadley, but he had to see her, make sure she really was alright. It was way after midnight and well after visiting hours, but he had friends in high places. The agent at the door had been called and was expecting Mike.

Mike slipped quietly into the room. There she was. Randi. She was lying on her back, covers twisted around her like she had been very restless. It would be a wonder if she didn't have nightmares from now on. His heart melted at her beauty. He traced her features with his eyes, the soft arch of her perfect brows, the hair making little curls around her small ears. The slant of her cheekbones. His gaze slid over to the softness of her lips, lips that looked luscious and at the same time very innocent. He wanted to press his lips against hers but he was afraid he might startle her. He didn't know yet what all she had been through. He prayed that she hadn't been harmed…but…

"Mike?" Randi's voice brought his eyes back to hers. Beautiful eyes.

"I'm so sorry. I didn't mean to wake you."

"Hey, it's okay. I wanted to see you, but I knew you were busy." She reached over and slid the back of her hand down his cheek. It was an intimate gesture. One she might not have made under different circumstances, but it touched him deep inside. He leaned his head sideways and pressed his lips against her soft hand. Her eyes were gleaming at him. They were so blue and clear. He could look into them forever and not get enough.

"Ahh…I…"

"Just spit it out, soldier," she laughed.

He laughed, as she had meant for him to.

"I want you to know that I like you, Randi Rae, and I'm going to try to get you to like me. Is that okay with you?" He reached for the hand that had stroked his cheek.

"Why, soldier, don't you know I already like you?"

It was all the encouragement he needed. He leaned closer and pressed his lips to hers in what was intended to be a quick chaste touch of lips, but turned into a full blown passionate kiss. When he pulled back a few moments later, he could tell Randi was as affected by the kiss as he was.

"Get some sleep. I'll come by early tomorrow. We need to talk."

Randi watched Mike leave, then pressed her fingers to her lips. She was still smiling as she drifted off to sleep.

CHAPTER 51

Five o'clock. Time to get moving. Tiger was ready for this takedown. All the agents were primed. They had the mission planned down to the second. Josh and Garrett were calling the shots. This was a very sensitive mission. One that he relished. He was just shy of thirty-two and had been a top agent for five years now. He had been in just about every country in the world on secret missions, some of which would never come to light. Black-ops missions. He had gone on some in conjunction with Navy SEALS, with the CIA, and a couple of other organizations he would not name. This was his life. No wife, no kids to worry about. That's the way he wanted it, he told himself.

Very few people knew his real name. He had an unusual background, one that he kept to himself. He kind of came and went like the wind. He was sent in to situations where they needed stealth. He got the job done and he left. No one knew where he went after a mission. He just seemed to disappear. He would reappear when needed for the next mission.

He watched as the other men bumped fists and checked equipment, getting each other and themselves psyched for the coming takedown. He didn't need that camaraderie. He didn't need to be psyched…it was as natural as breathing to him.

"Move out." Josh and Garrett watched as the men pulled on their gear and exited the room. Each one knew their job and would do what needed done. They went over to the window to watch as the van and cars pulled away from the Field Office.

"Are we doing the right thing? Making the whole thing a public spectacle? A scandal? Maybe we should let him just get out of the country. Tell the people that he died of a massive stroke? Wouldn't it be better for the country?"

"We can't make those judgments, Garrett. We have to do our jobs. Let the justice system do its job."

"Will the Supreme Court have to decide how to proceed with the election, or what?"

"I don't know how that works. Bummer." Josh hated all this. It was hard enough around election time anyway. He wished he was home with his beautiful wife. Wished his daughter would forgive him and come by more often. He missed their close relationship. Today was one of those days that made it difficult to get up and go to work. Seeing all the corruption in peoples' lives. Hadley, Peeves, the man who had done the kidnapping. They had found his body in a shallow grave someone's dog had dug up. The dog's owner had freaked out when the dog began pulling a man's hand out of the pile of dirt. The police had called it in to the FBI because of the physical description of the man matched the one given by Randi as her kidnapper.

"Not there. How can he not be there? The agents watched him go in and nobody has come out of the apartment since then. How did he evade his Secret Service agents, anyway?"

"Josh." Garrett listened on the phone for a moment as the agent explained the situation they found at Hadley's apartment.

"There's a man here, apparently some derelict Hadley paid to switch places with him. It had to have happened in the elevator or a hallway on the way to his apartment. The man was instructed what to wear and he was to stay in the apartment all night." The agent relayed a message from Charlie, the agent in charge at the scene, that it looked like most of Hadley's things were missing.

He must have prepared ahead of time. Was someone feeding him information?

"Wrap it up. Bring the man back with you and put him in one of the interrogation rooms." Garrett closed his phone and sat down heavily on the sofa, leaning his head back against the soft leather.

"I've got some explaining to do to the Chief-of-Staff and to the President." Josh spoke the thoughts rumbling around in Garrett's head.

"Yeah, good luck." Garrett grinned back at Josh.

"Chicken. You mean you don't have my back?"

"Sure. I have your back. Just a long way back."

Josh studied his friend and fellow agent. They were totally different in looks and a lot in temperament, but they got on very well.

To have such opposing jobs in different areas, Secret Service and FBI, they worked well together. Within the scope of what they were allowed they even shared information.

"Hey. You know I'm just fooling. 'Course I'll be there."

Mike left the FBI Field Office soon after Josh and Garrett confirmed that Hadley had gotten away. They assured him that Randi was safe, but they would make sure she had a bodyguard and someone assigned to watch her house. They wanted to do the same for him but he refused. He was well trained to look after himself and would be extra cautious until they knew Hadley's whereabouts. It shouldn't be long. Every airport and train station in a five state area was being monitored, along with the Canadian and Mexican borders. The Coast Guard was keeping an eye on all boats leaving the many marinas scattered along the coast.

Randi had agreed to let Mike pick her up from the hospital. Will had offered and so had Dan and Jeff, but she thought they understood. She was pretty transparent when it came to her feelings for Mike. When she had woken up and seen his face hovering above hers she felt such a joy. She had wanted to throw herself in his arms and never let go. If she hadn't been half asleep she probably would have.

It was when he had kissed the back of her hand with such tenderness and he touched his lips to the ragged sores on her wrist that she had fallen head-over-heels in love with him. She was a goner from that moment on.

"Ready to go?" Mike brushed a curl from her forehead and let his fingers linger on her cheek.

Randi raised up from the bed where she had been waiting, gathered her purse and the small bag her mother had brought to her. Mike reached out and enfolded her small hand in his much larger one. She felt safer than she had since all this started.

CHAPTER 52

"Mr. President." Josh and Garrett were seated with several members of the President's closest staff members, the Head of White House Security, Daniel Marlow, and Paul, the President's Chief-of-Staff. Josh felt under the circumstances that Mike should be there. But Marlow stated that Calloway's security clearance did not reach that level. The President had to agree, even though he really liked the young man.

"Get to it Josh. What happened with Hadley? I was told something was going down, but I didn't get all the info because of the situation in Israel. If it's something you two can handle, please do so, and let me get back to work. I'm trying to handle the election stuff and this situation and I have little free time."

"Hadley is not in the running for the presidency any longer." That got Cole's attention.

"What? What happened?" Cole looked at his Chief-of-Staff. "Paul?"

"I think it would be better if we let Josh answer that question."

Josh took a deep breath and let it out slowly. He hated throwing this at the president, especially this close to the election he had worked so hard for.

"Mr. President, we uncovered something in Horace Hadley's past that has made it impossible for him to continue to pursue the office of president."

"I see," he said, even though he didn't. What could have been there that the media wouldn't have uncovered? Truthfully, he was just stunned. He couldn't process what all this meant.

"Sir, we're pretty sure Hadley was involved in the shooting of Mike Calloway and in the kidnapping of Randi Rae." Josh let that sink in for a moment before he went on. "This whole thing began back over ten years ago." He stopped to make sure he had the President's attention.

"Ten years?"

"Yes, there were some compromising photographs of Hadley…"

"Stop right there. We're not going to get in a slinging match over some hyped up photos. I know he was behind those faked pictures of my wife and…" he didn't want to finish that thought, "but we are not going to play that game, understood?"

"Sir, just please hear us out. It's not the same thing. These photos were taken ten years ago and they show a murder in progress. The murder of Mathias Garvey, a Chief of Police in your hometown. Hadley is the one holding the gun."

Cole remembered. He was a District Attorney at the time. No one was ever arrested for that. It remained a cold case. His attention hadn't been on that much because that was the same time he had lost his son. His beautiful, precious son. He did remember that Horace Hadley had accepted the promotion opened by the former Chief of Police's death. That started Hadley on his upward climb professionally.

"How did you get hold of these photos? Especially after all this time? Do you know if they're genuine? Have you had them checked out?"

"Yes, sir." Garrett answered that question. "We had the best techs double check everything. They've not been tampered with. They show a little yellowing, but that's because they were in the camera for a couple of years before being processed."

"Why so long?" Cole's suspicions were still on high alert.

"We haven't quite got to all that yet, but we will, sir. Josh called Mike. He's coming in to talk with us."

"Mike?"

"Mike Calloway, sir. He's the one who took the pictures."

"Nice young man. He took the pictures, you say?" At Garrett's nod, Cole thought about it a moment. "This Mike – he's young. Twenty-six, right?" Another nod.

"I think that's right, sir."

"That would make him about sixteen when he took the photos. Why didn't he come forward with them at the time?"

"Maybe he can answer those questions when he gets here, sir."

CHAPTER 53

Cam should hate Mike Calloway for taking his place as son to his parents. Yet he just couldn't hate him. In some ways he was even grateful that his parents had someone there for them. A son that they could nurture and love. It was Cam's own fault. All the trouble he had been in when he was young and stupid. He had done so much. He took a few drugs. Ran with the wrong crowd, a terrible crowd. He had never killed anyone, but he had watched someone be killed. That's what woke him up. He secretly went to the authorities…turned state's evidence to the FBI. He was seventeen at the time. He had a choice to make. He could go back to his parents and beg their forgiveness and be their son again, making them a target for the men he had turned in, or he could stay away and start a new life, get his act right. He decided on the latter. A couple of the FBI guys seemed to really like him. They got him a job, helped him get his GED, and even helped him get into a good college. He repaid them by being the best FBI SWAT agent he could be.

The FBI agents that helped him had become not only his mentors but his best friends. One of them, Garrett Sullivan, was now Director of the FBI.

He had seen Mike Calloway from a distance, but not met him. Maybe he should introduce himself. See if maybe they could be friendly, at least. He didn't know how this Mike would take it, finding out his parents' real son was alive. He didn't plan on making any trouble for Mike.

Mike wanted to stay with Randi, but he could tell she wouldn't relax and get some sleep as long as he hung around. He left her after she promised to stay put, and let her bodyguards know if she needed anything or if she had any calls that bothered her. Before leaving her. He couldn't help it – he pressed a quick soft kiss to her beautiful lips and was out the door before tempted to repeat it.

The FBI Field Office was teeming when Mike got there. The SWAT team member that had taken Randi to the hospital approached him as he looked for the main conference room.

"It's this way. Everybody's in there cooling their heels, waiting on some kind of lead to work on." Mike turned toward the room he indicated, but turned back to thank the man for taking care of Randi.

"Thank you. I'm sorry, I don't know your name…"

Cam looked into Mike's eyes. "Mike, I'm Cam."

"Cam?" Mike looked at the man. Was he supposed to know him?

"Cam Calloway." Cam saw realization dawn on Mike, but was unprepared for being enveloped a bear hug.

"Cam, Cam Calloway. My God, your parents thought you were probably dead. It's…it's wonderful to meet you. But why? Why no word in all those years?"

The accusation seared into his being. It was justified. He should have at least let them know he was alive.

"Mike, by the time I woke up from being stupid, it was just too late. At first I did it to protect them, then when I could have gone to them, I found out they had been killed."

"You men coming in or what?" The meeting was starting.

"Cam. We need to talk." Cam nodded and walked into the conference room.

"Later, Mike. I'll call you, okay?"

"Listen up, everyone. This meeting is for your ears only. No gossip outside. None." Josh looked at each man. Memorizing who was there. He didn't think there would be any problems with leaking information. He knew everyone here and they were all good men, but he had to warn them anyway, for the record.

"Once the president is online with the meeting, we'll get started."

"This meeting is for the president to get caught up on everything that's happened so far. As you know he's been pretty busy keeping things from escalating in the Middle East." One of the techs motioned to Josh that they were ready.

A picture started forming on the screen and then morphed into the president sitting in the White House conference room. Several top security men were with him as well as Paul, his Chief of Staff, and the head of White House Security, Daniel Marlow. Mel Myers sat to the president's left.

"Okay, men. We're on." Josh faced the screen, "Hello, Mr. President. We're ready."

"Good, Josh. Why don't you start from the beginning and I'll hold my questions until I have a better grasp of the situation."

"Actually, Mr. President, I think Mike would be better starting us off. The photos date back ten years and Mike was the one who took them."

"Alright. Mike, how are you doing now?"

"I'm doing fine, Mr. President. I'm sorry. I wish I hadn't brought all this on you."

"Not your fault, son. Hadley is the one who should take all the blame here."

"There are only a limited number of things I can tell you, sir. I had the camera in my possession for a couple of years and had forgotten about it. I found it in my things when I came back from college, and realized it had undeveloped film in it. I had it developed, but I didn't understand what the photos were. I just felt they were important for some reason, so I kept them in a safe place. I didn't know where to go with them."

"Did you recognize any of the men in the photos?"

"No, sir."

"Go on."

"I know you're aware of the situation with me being shot." At the President's nod he continued. "It was after that I had a run in with the same man who had fired that shot. He tried to kill me in a back alley a couple of weeks later. Claimed I should've died the first time he tried to kill me. It had embarrassed him not to finish the job he was paid for. The FBI got very little information out of him before he was murdered in the hospital. It was just a few days later that Randi Rae was kidnapped."

"What does her kidnapping have to do with this?" Cole was getting confused.

"They were using her to get to me, sir. Somehow they knew they could get what they wanted from me if they had her. I was contacted on my cell phone by someone who had their voice distorted. They told me to bring the photos to the park, all copies and negatives, or Randi would die. They told me not to contact any authorities, but they didn't know DeeAnn had already alerted everyone when she talked to Randi and got really bad vibes about her being late to their meeting."

"Okay, so you're saying this was all Hadley's doing because of the photos."

"That's what we figure, sir."

"And these photos…you took them?"

"I-I think so, sir. I had the camera in my pocket when…"

"When what, son?"

Mike looked around the room. There were too many people here. He couldn't talk about some of this. This was his whole life he was revealing.

"Sir, could I talk with you privately about that part?"

"I don't think this is the time to be hesitant, son. Just spill it."

Mike took a deep breath. This could change his whole life. Could he be court marshaled for lying to the military…to the president?

"Sir. The camera was in my pocket when I met the Calloways. I don't know how it got there or how long I had it. I can't remember anything that happened before I woke up in the Calloways' RV ten years ago.

"The Calloways. They are not your parents?'

"No, sir. They sort of… adopted me, sir."

"And why's that? Why can't you remember?" Cole was beginning to have the strangest feeling in his chest.

"Where did you grow up, son?"

"I don't know. I just know I woke up in Micah and Marian Calloway's RV somewhere in Arizona. I couldn't tell them anything and they didn't know where to start to find out anything about me."

Josh was staring at him and it made him nervous. Was he going to press charges against him? Mike tried to focus on what the president was asking, but his head was beginning to hurt.

"Ten years ago, you said. That would have made you sixteen, right?"

"Uh…no, sir. I can remember one or two things, now. I would have been twelve at the time, sir. I'm twenty-two, not twenty-six." He could hear the rumble in the room starting low but getting louder.

Cole felt the room start to whirl. *Could it be? I would never have considered the possibility. Could that be why this young man has seemed so familiar to me?*

"Josh. Get here now! And bring Mike Calloway with you." Cole signaled the technician to shut down the video feed. He could hear the murmuring around the room. He let it pass without comment.

"Where's my wife?" He searched the room for his Chief-of-Staff.

Paul Romero was worried about the president. He looked so pale. "Are you okay, sir?"

"Paul, where is Celeste?"

"I believe she's is still at that conference for women she goes to every year. She's supposed to speak there in about an hour."

"Get her here as soon as she makes her speech, okay? And find my girls. I want them here, too."

"Sir, if I may ask, what's going on?" Paul had never seen Cole act like this.

"I'll fill you in later. It may be nothing, then again it might be something very, very big." He looked over at his friend of so many years. "Mel." Mel knew what he was thinking. "Come with me." Cole turned and walked out of the office heading for his private quarters.

CHAPTER 54

Celeste was exhausted. The conference had been wonderful. Even DeeAnn and Brooke enjoyed it. She had decided it was time they learned to extend themselves. Not just think about their lives and their wants but reach out to the community, to others, some in desperate need of food, clothing, or shelter. Some just needed to know they weren't alone. That someone cared.

She didn't expect to be pulled from the meeting early. Worry for her husband was always foremost in her mind. He had such a burden, and the last few weeks had been even more stressful than usual.

"Hello, darlings." Surprised that her other daughters, Dolly and Madeline, were all in the sitting room at this time of day, she hugged each one and asked, "Why are you all here? Dolly, I thought you had a buyer to meet this morning. Is everything okay?"

"Mom, we don't know. We were contacted and told Daddy wanted us all to meet him here. No one said what it was about."

"I'm scared, Mom. He's never done this before." Brooke slid her arms around her mother's waist, and

Celeste automatically put her arms around her youngest daughter's slight frame.

"Everything will be fine, sweetheart. You know God is in control still, right?"

Brooke looked up into her mother's smiling eyes and drew from her strength.

"Yeah, I'd forgotten that. Thanks, Mom."

The door opened and Cole walked in to find his family gathered like a small army set to do battle for him. No tears, no whining about why their days had been interrupted. He was so proud of them, but the news he had would have to wait for a few hours. He had wanted his family with him so when the media storm hit they would already know and not get blindsided. The one that was going to get blindsided would be Mike Calloway, but it couldn't be helped. This had to be done quietly and quickly.

Mel walked in a minute later. "Everything is in progress, Cole."

"Cole?" Celeste reached for her husband's hand. It was cold as ice. Now *she* was afraid.

"Celeste, girls, let's sit a while." Cole walked to the sofa, bringing his wife with him. He pulled her close to him as he sat down.

"How was the conference?" He had to smile at his wife's expression. This was not going to be easy for any of them. They knew he was stalling.

"The conference was going well." She raised one eyebrow, playing along with his tactics. She knew her husband well. The look of strain around his eyes let her know something was brewing.

"Girls? Did you enjoy the conference? Learn a lot?"

"Daddy?" DeeAnn spoke for her and Brooke. "Yes, we did enjoy it. It was better than we expected. I'll probably go next year, too. But ..."

"No buts...just humor me for a while, okay? Small talk for now. Dolly, how did your meeting go?"

Dolly picked up on the vibes her Dad was giving off. "It was very productive. I hope to have some new offerings in the near future that will help get our name out over more area." She relaxed back in her chair and began reeling off different projects they were working on. Small talk to help pass the time until whatever her father was waiting on happened. Madeline helped by asking some leading questions and her mom joined in. DeeAnn and Brooke just tried to follow the conversations and not ask the questions they were bursting to ask.

The president spoke several times with his chief advisors on the situation in the Middle East. It was a nice family time, even though it was a little edgy still.

Three hours after they had gathered in the sitting room, Cole took the call that would change his and his family's life forever. It was a match.

"Mike. What's it all about?" Randi had been sitting in the apartment, talking with Mike and getting to know him a little better. She knew what she felt for Mike was more than just attraction. She just didn't know a lot about him and that needed to change before things got too complicated.

He'd tried to explain to her about his loss of memory, but it was hard for her to grasp. She had a hard time accepting that he couldn't remember his parents or where he grew up. Those things were like breath to her. Family and belonging. History.

He searched her beautiful eyes, trying to gage how much this was going to affect their relationship. A relationship that was so new and delicate, it might not survive this trauma.

"I…I can't tell you a whole lot more because I just don't remember, and I don't know why."

"The bullet they took out – you think that's why you can't remember?"

"I guess it's possible, since I don't remember even how that happened." Mike pulled her closer to him on the sofa, just needing to have her close.

"Can you tell me what the meeting is about with the president?" She knew there was only so much he could say about the Hadley thing. They were still looking for him. She couldn't believe that man had used her to get to Mike.

"I really don't know. Josh just said to be ready for him to call, and then be ready to be picked up for the meeting. I'm not sure why the delay unless the president has other more important business to take care of."

"Uh, go figure. More important business?" He laughed, as she knew he would.

Josh's phone call came a little before six that evening. By that time everyone's nerves were on edge. Jeff and Will had come in. Mike explained as much as he could to them about the situation with Hadley. Randi told them of the meeting with the president, and by that time Josh was at the door ready to escort Mike to the White House.

As Mike turned to say goodbye, Randi was right behind him. He put his hands on her shoulders and just scanned her face with his eyes. He had the eerie feeling that he might not ever see her again. He tilted her face up to his and planted a soft kiss to her lips. There were tears in her eyes as he turned to follow Josh down the steps and into the waiting limo.

Josh didn't say much as they drove from the apartment where Mike lived to the White House. He was as much in the dark as Mike was, and he really didn't want to show it. Something major was going on. This...this seemed to be personal.

"Mike, you know what's going on?" He hated to ask, but if Mike did know he wanted that information so he could be prepared.

Mike glanced his way. He couldn't tell, but Mike looked puzzled.

"You don't know? I was hoping you would tell me. This is strange. Am I in trouble?"

"Why would you think you might be in trouble?"

"Mr. Key..."

"Josh, please."

"Josh, I've lied to the military, the president, you name it. I've pretended to be someone I'm not. That's enough for a court martial."

"Maybe. There are extenuating circumstances, though. Those will be taken into consideration. The only thing I know is that the vice-president called and said to bring you to see the president in his personal quarters." He passed through the White House security points with a wave of his credentials and the necessary scan underneath the car. He just hoped what he was telling Mike would be the truth. He really liked the young man. But he could be in a world of trouble if the media caught any whiff of the story. They would tear him apart.

Mike looked around as he was led to the President's sitting room. He had been there a few times after that first interview to pick up Brooke and sometimes DeeAnn, and the time he had lunch with the first lady and all the girls. Now he felt more nervous, if possible, than he had on that first interview. Why was he meeting the president in his personal space and not in one of the conference rooms?

CHAPTER 55

Celeste had not been prepared for her husband's words. Sean…alive? All the air seemed to rush out of the room. She couldn't have heard him right. She heard the gasp from Madeline and a squeak from Brooke. Dolly was the first to speak.

"Dad, is this one of those guys who has come to you claiming to be Sean after that appeal to the media for information? If it is, I don't want to know about it. And I don't think you should jump to any conclusions this quickly." Always the protective one, she didn't want her mother or her sisters' hopes up just to find out it was a well-executed hoax.

"Honey, I know. You girls and your mother will have to trust me. I had the labs do an extremely rushed job on this. I know it's possible it may not be true. The results are not final. That takes time to sort out. But the preliminary results are so close, almost perfect. I can't leave you in the dark on this in case…" On that last he hesitated.

Madeline searched her father's face. "In case what, Dad?"

"Ahem." He felt like a boulder was lodged in his throat and had to take a minute to swallow to try and loosen it.

"In case the media get some wind of what's going on. You know how they are and I want you at least prepared to deal with it. I don't want you hit with it and not have a clue." He reached to take his wife's hand. "I know how hard it will be if it turns out he is not our Sean, but I've always been open with you and the girls as far as my ability to do so. I can tell you what's going on with Hadley. That will hit by tonight's news. I will have to get a statement together for some time tomorrow. Hadley is out of the race."

"Cole! How? What happened? Is he ill?"

"Sweetheart. You are so tenderhearted. No he's not sick, unless you count soul sick. We have indication, good indication, of his involvement in a murder that happened ten years ago."

"Wow. That's crazy." As DeeAnn moved close to her dad, he pulled her against his side and placed his arm around her waist.

"I know, honey. It's going to get crazier. Can I count on you girls to pull together and help your mom deal with the storm?"

"Absolutely, dad. Our prayer vigil starts now." Dolly grabbed Brooke's hand and her mother's hand, and the rest linked hands until they had a full circle.

With heads bowed Cole led them in a prayer for strength and healing, a prayer for the nation because of the turmoil of the election status. He prayed for the young man who would be walking through those doors in a few minutes.

"Cole, who is this man who you believe is our son? Is it someone we've met?" She answered her own question, "Surely not...or I would've recognized him. Wouldn't I?"

Cole hated that she sounded so upset. She would be more upset knowing how close she had been. He couldn't believe it either. He would have thought he would recognize his own son, even after ten years, but he had changed so much. And if you're not expecting it you may not see it. Besides, he thought Mike was twenty-six. It was only after Mike said he was really twenty-two that everything just seemed to click.

"Celeste..." A knock at the door cut off the rest of his sentence.

Mike hesitated at the door to the sitting room. His heart was pounding and he felt a little light-headed. *Oh man*. He hoped he didn't throw up in front of the president. Taking a deep breath, he let it out slowly and stepped through the door.

The scene that greeted him was surprising. All the president's family was sitting there staring at him, including the president, himself.

"Mike, come in. We need to talk." Mike came closer to the president, shook his hand, and nodded at the rest of the Harris family. They were looking at him with wide eyes and stunned expressions. He was getting all kinds of vibes from them that he couldn't process. He looked at each of the President's daughters. He had met Madeline a few times, but didn't know her very well.

On her face was a look between a scowl and a smile. A strange expression. Dolly frowned and DeeAnn just looked mad. Brooke…Brooke was smiling the biggest smile he had ever seen on her face.

"Mike," Mrs. Harris's voice sounded almost strangled. "Come here, please."

He came close to her, took the hand she held out, and caught her just before she hit the floor in a dead faint.

"Mom!" All four girls rushed forward at the same time.

"Celeste!" Cole reached out for his wife but allowed Mike to pick her up and carry her to the sofa. "Brooke, call security and get them to send for medical attention."

"No…no…I'm fine." Celeste was coming around and trying to rise up, but Mike was holding her back with gentle pressure to one shoulder.

"Please, take it easy. At least until we know you're okay." Mike eased the pressure on her shoulder as she lay back against the arm of the plush sofa. He could see her right hand shaking as she reached and put it against his left cheek. A charge, almost like electricity, seemed to flow from her hand to sting his cheek.

He jerked. He could tell she felt it, too.

"What…" She shushed him.

"Just let me look at you." He could almost feel her eyes as she assessed each feature of his face. He felt the tremble in her fingers as she swept them across his brow. What were the others thinking as this went on? He could feel the rising heat of embarrassment creep up his neck.

"Mike," President Harris gently drew Mike into a standing position with a firm hand around his arm. "There's a lot to talk about. If you'll sit with the girls, we'll get things sorted out. Celeste, are you okay, sweetheart?"

She nodded her head yes, not trusting her voice. She sat up and moved to the side so the girls and Mike would have room.

"If you would bear with us and answer a few questions?" Cole waited for Mike's response.

"I…of course, sir." This was getting stranger by the minute. Brooke sat close beside him on his left side and DeeAnn close on his right. Madeline opted to sit in the chair next to the sofa. Dolly sat on a cushion on the floor beside Madeline.

"Tell me about the photos and anything you can remember about that time. Anything about yourself."

"But, sir, I've told you I don't remember…"

"I know you don't remember much. Just humor me, okay?"

Mike began telling the story of his life with the Calloways. How he woke up in their RV in the middle of the Arizona desert, the only things in his possession being the clothes he was wearing and the camera in his pocket. He told of his schooling, his faked birth certificate, his early entrance into college and then into the military. He didn't mention anything about the money his "parents" had left him or of the insurance money that was still sitting in the bank in California.

He sighed as he finished and shrugged, "That's it. The rest you pretty much know except for what happened yesterday and today with Horace Hadley."

"And we'll leave that for the news. I've given them the general scope of the deal with Hadley and how it's going to affect the election." Cole reached over and pulled a chair close and sat down with a heavy sigh. "What I want to ask you now are the few things you remember. You said that after you had been with the Calloways for about three months, they provided a birth certificate in order for you to get a driver's license? And that spurred a memory at the time?"

"Yes, sir. I…"

"It's okay, son, you're not in any trouble. We just need a little information, as best you can remember."

"I remembered that I was twelve, sir. They thought I was close to the age of their son who would've been sixteen at the time. I was big for my age, I guess. Anyway, I remembered only after they got the certificate. It couldn't be changed. So I remained sixteen by the certificate. Got my license, went to college two years later, into the military two years after that. I don't know how to fix it, sir."

"It's not your fault, son. Circumstances happen. We'll get it fixed." He wanted nothing more than to take this young man in his arms and erase all the years that had been lost. He wished he could meet the Calloways, thank them for taking care of his son and making him the fine young man that he was.

"Mike, have you ever tried to find out who you really are?"

At the question, the old fears leaped to life. Why? He knew now why he had been so afraid. He had witnessed a murder and the murderer had come after him. He should be over the fear. The murderer had found him and, yet, he had survived.

"I guess the irrational fear that it was the police chasing me. Some of the men in the photos were police officers. I never wanted the Calloways to take me to the police. I talked them out of it because my fear was so overwhelming since I didn't know who to trust."

Cole took a deep breath before asking the next question. "If you could find out, would you want to?"

"Sir, I just don't know. How fair would it be to them?" He felt sadder than he could ever remember. A lump started to form in his throat. Would he never remember where he came from? Never know if he was Irish or German or English heritage. If he ever had children, what would he be able to tell them about their grandparents?

"I'm sorry, I don't understand. How would it be unfair? Wouldn't they be overjoyed at finding their son?"

"If their son couldn't remember them, how happy would they be?" Mike stood and moved off to the window. "I used to daydream about them finding me and me remembering everything. I gave up on that long ago. I just don't think that will ever happen. Maybe because of the head trauma that bullet caused. I'm pretty sure from everything I've learned in the last two days that Hadley was responsible for the bullet they found in my head. Besides, wouldn't they have looked for me? I mean, wouldn't they have hired someone to keep searching for me? Maybe they didn't really care. Maybe they had several other kids and just weren't that interested in finding one who could bring trouble to them.

He heard a sound to his left and saw Mrs. Harris wiping the tears from her cheeks. It pained him to see those tears and he hoped it wasn't anything he did or said that caused them.

"Mike, I want you to listen very carefully to me. I think I speak for my wife as well as for my daughters." He checked with each one and each gave a nod for him to go on. Dolly reached over and squeezed her father's hand.

"I think your family would feel truly blessed just to know the man you have become. If in time other memories came, so much the better, but they would love you for who you are now."

"How could I be sure, though? I wouldn't want to intrude on their lives."

"I know who you are, Mike. I know where you come from, and I know your family." Cole let that sink in for a moment.

"Your name is Sean Harris. You are our son." Nobody moved. Nobody spoke.

Mike looked not at Cole but at Celeste, and he knew. Knew it was true. The feelings he had when he first met her. This was his mom. He couldn't speak, couldn't even breath. His eyes searched her face. Where were the memories, the memories of her holding him when he was afraid, of her waking him up for school in the mornings, of Christmas and Thanksgiving? Why couldn't he remember? Not being able to pull from those images of the past, how was he supposed to know how to feel? Just as it felt like his insides were being torn out piece by piece, soft arms closed around him and it felt like coming home.

"You don't have to remember everything, or anything for that matter. We already know many things about you, from your past and from your present. We're…we're just so happy you're alive, that's all." Tears streamed down her face but they couldn't dim the glorious smile.

"Celeste, let the boy breathe." Cole laughed. He felt like the sun was shining after a long, dark winter. A knot had formed in his throat as he watched his wife and son. He didn't know what the future would bring, but right now life was wonderful. The whole family was together again after ten long heartbreaking years.

CHAPTER 56

They stayed up talking well past midnight. Mike told them the other thing he had remembered was that he had sisters. He just couldn't remember how many or anything about them.

"Well, we'll just have to rectify that." At a look from her dad, Madeline went on. "Whenever you're ready, let us know, okay?" He looked toward Madeline. There was a flash of memory, but he couldn't grasp it before it was gone. Still, it gave him hope. He'd had so few memory flashes over the years. Maybe that was because he hadn't wanted to remember. He had been too afraid. Maybe now, if he tried, he could begin to remember more.

"Tell me about where we lived. Where I went to school. Who was my best friend? I have so many questions."

"We'll answer whatever you want to know, but Mi… Sean, please, take it easy, okay? We have plenty of time. Don't try to force the memories, okay?

A family. My family. His heart felt like it was about to burst.

"I guess I better go. There's going to be a lot going on tomorrow." He hated to leave his family when he'd just found them. "I'll come by?" It was formed as a question.

Cole stood up when Mike did. "I'll get security to fix you up with clearance to come and go. Son, I…" he couldn't finish the sentence.

Mike had intended to shake his father's hand, but somehow they both just wrapped their arms about each other in a tight hug. The flash of pain in his head didn't register at first. All thought of the present fled and he was a twelve-year-old boy again.

CHAPTER 57

The FBI was not able to locate Horace Hadley. The Secret Service and the FBI would continue to search for any information they could find, but it wasn't looking very promising the more time went by. He had to have had help getting away or he had to have had plans in place beforehand. They checked the street cameras for anyone who could possibly be him even in disguise. Nothing. If he left the country, they couldn't find where or how but they weren't giving up. More information had come in about the pictures and what they meant. Two of the other men who were identified by the photographs had been contacted and were being questioned about their part in the killing. They told the FBI how Hadley had coerced them into helping him kill Mathias Garvey so he could move up into the man's position.

Mathias Garvey was a much loved and respected Chief of Police in Richmond, Virginia. He had been in the position for almost ten years and was not looking to move up from the position. He loved the job and the people he worked with. He was young enough – only forty-one – that he could be there many more years. This did not suit Horace Hadley's plans at all. Horace was a senior officer and wanted to move up to Chief of Police. It was his plan to use that office to get him closer to a Senate seat and eventually to the presidency. He didn't care whom he had to step on or threaten in order to get what he wanted.

By killing Garvey, Hadley had been able to advance into the position. After a few years as Chief of Police, Hadley had run for the Senate and by some dirty politics had gotten the seat. That was three years ago. Now he had launched his campaign to be President.

That wasn't going to happen. If he ever showed his face in public again, he would be arrested for murder.

EPILOGUE

There was a wedding in the works. Mike who had decided to remain as Mike but take his real last name of Harris, had finally asked Randi to marry him. It had taken a couple of months for things to settle down after the election.

Now, with Cole's re-election, the wedding reception would be in the White House ballroom. He had held off telling the people of his son. He didn't want it to seem like he was using that as a playing card to sway the election. With the announcement of the wedding, he was ready to show off his son to the whole world.

"Mike." Randi looked up at her husband-to-be. He was so good looking it took her breath away, and when he reached for her hand, she slipped naturally into his arms. The wedding was only two weeks away, but it seemed like forever. The fact that he was the president's son just amazed and frightened her. She would be a part of the presidential family. *Wow*. She had been friends with the girls for several years, but this was different. She hoped DeeAnn was okay with it. She hadn't really had a chance to talk to her for a few weeks. It had been so crazy after the abduction, and then Mike had told her about his connection with the Harris family. And then the wedding announcement.

"I love you," he stated and then proved it with a kiss that took what remaining breath she had away.

"And I love you." Her eyes shone with a mist of tears.

"And that makes you cry?" he teased.

"Oh, you know women do that. Better get used to it. You'll see a lot of them at the wedding."

"About that…"

"Oh, no you don't. You're not backing out now. The invitations have been sent. A week ago." She was teasing, too, but she must have had a worried look on her face enough to convince him.

"Honey, I would never back out. You've got me, like it or not." Then he kissed her with a passion he had never shown before, and she almost swooned at his feet.

Mike's life had changed so much over the past few months. He had a family again. A family who loved him. There had been no reason for him to worry if his family cared. They loved him the whole time and had suffered so much when they thought he was gone forever.

Now, in a couple of weeks he would be adding a beautiful bride to his family. A woman he loved more and more every day. He felt God's blessings on his life and thanked Him for taking care of Randi and prayed that he would be a good husband, and, hopefully one day, a good father to their children.

Children. I'm not even married yet and I'm already thing about our children. It was okay, though. He and Randi talked over all the major points and were amazed at how in tune they were with each other. Of course Jeff and Will joked around with him, telling him they wouldn't let him out of his lease for another seven months. He and Randi would have to live in the apartment with Jeff and Will until the lease was up. The president called them and they backed off in a hurry. It was all in fun.

Mike asked them to be groomsmen in the wedding. They accepted with smiles and pats on the back. Randi figured he would ask Charlie to be his best man, but Mike had other plans. He intended to ask Cam. When Mike told Randi about the SWAT team leader being the Calloways' real son, she was amazed at the way God works. She remembered how Cam had taken care of her after her ordeal, how gentle he was with her. She thought it was a wonderful idea.

Mike picked up his mail from the table by the door as soon as he entered the apartment. His mail had picked up considerably since he was now known as the president's son. If he didn't stay on top of it, it accumulated way too fast. A couple of bills. Yeah, being the son of the president didn't stop the bills from coming. An invitation to take out so-and-so's credit card. No thanks. An invitation to Dolly and Louis's gallery for a showing. He set that to one side. He definitely wanted to go to that.

This one has no name or return address. Probably slipped into my box since there's no postage on it. Hmm.

As soon as he opened the little card, he knew it was trouble.

Pay day...some day!

HH